THE BEAST HUNTERS

First published in Great Britain by Hashtag Press 2021
This edition published in Norway by 2022
Text © Christer Lende 2022
Cover Design © Andrei Bat 2022

All rights reserved. No part of this publication may be reproduced, stored in retrieval system, or transmitted, in any form or by any means without the prior written permission of the publisher, nor be otherwise circulated in any form of binding or cover other than that in which it is published and without a similar condition being imposed on the subsequent purchaser.

All characters in this publication are fictitious and any resemblance to actual persons, living or dead, is purely coincidental.

ISBN 979-83-593165-4-5

THE BEAST HUNTERS

Christer Lende

C. A. Lende Publishing

DEDICATION

*This book is dedicated to my late grandfather, Ragnar Fanebust, who spent his life with a pen in hand.
He would be proud.*

ALSO BY

CHRISTER LENDE

THE BEAST HUNTER OF ASHBOURN SERIES:
The Beast Hunters
The Beast Hunters Dark Sovereign
The Beast Hunters Blood Oath

The Dollmaker of Kalastra
Bleeding Ink

SIGN UP FOR MY AUTHOR NEWSLETTER

Be the first to find out all the super-duper exciting news about Christer Lende's new releases and life, and get some free short stories while you're at it: https://www.authorcalende.com/newsletter-signup

ACKNOWLEDGEMENTS

Firstly, I would like to thank my mother, Anette Lende. She had nothing to do with this book, but *did* give birth to me, so thank you for that.

A huge thanks goes out to my editors as well, Tiffany Schmidt, Anna Windgatter, and C. D. Tavenor.

I want to thank my girlfriend of ten years, Emma Kristine Skjæveland, for always supporting me, despite never reading a single word.

Nicole Schramm was the first person ever to read the full story and gave me a lot of motivation.

A close second was Tom Haugen, who devoured all three books in a week or so.

Ole-Marius Skulbru was the first person ever to lay his eyes upon any part of this book and his instant praise for it kept me going in the beginning.

Sin Jace Blix-Torres read the book in less than a day, and I can't thank you enough. It was a wild ride and led to great conversations.

First, he was my personal trainer, then we became friends, then he became my boss, and ultimately now he is an incredibly important person in my life, Jared Trevor Lea-Smith. Thanks for reading.

Tom Christian Klingsheim is a good friend of mine, but he said it as true as it is: you never really believe that any close friends can actually write great books. Luckily, he ate those words willingly after reading this.

My little sister, Kaja Lende, had to read a book for school, and chose her brother's book. That way, when she had to answer questions about 'what the author really meant' she could get it straight from the source.

Jonatan Dam read the book too and demanded at a party that I put him in here. Are you happy now? No need for threats.

A thanks also goes out to Gord Kverme, who read the exact amount of the book I said he had to read, to get into the acknowledgments.

THE RURA

Supper was cold by the time Ara got to eat. Her mother, Nadia, had made her restack the timber outside the house, which had taken until sundown. Ara found it peculiar that it had fallen over. Her father blamed the night's strong winds, but Ara knew the night had been calm because she hadn't slept.

Her body still bore marks from the beating her father had given her the day before, when he'd stumbled over her misplaced shoe. She had no idea how it ended up on his bedroom doorstep, but he didn't believe her. Though no one was in the messy old kitchen, she tried to cover the bruises with her tattered shirt, tucking it around her while slouching in the chair. She hated how they made her body look.

Despite being cold, the soup tasted good; Ara was so hungry that anything would have done. The small portion went down quickly, luckily before either of her parents walked into the kitchen, disrupting her peace with more chores. She cleaned up after herself and set the bowl down as quietly as she could.

No reason to antagonise either of them.

There it was, that faint sour smell. *Is it me?* She sniffed her armpits. But the scent disappeared as quickly as it had appeared.

Nadia entered the small kitchen, tugging on her long dark hair with one hand as she always did when stressed.

With her other hand, she began to search through drawers. Ara sat quietly, hoping her mother would leave her alone. Nadia found a dirty washcloth and returned to the living room, without a glance at her daughter. Ara sighed in relief. Her mother wasn't as harsh as her father, Tom, and sometimes they even laughed together, but around her father, Nadia was subservient. "There it is again," her father said, annoyed, from the living room.

The door between the two rooms used to shield her from his sight when she ate alone, but it had broken off its last hinge. Luckily, a damp newspaper with faded print was in his hands. She dreaded the very thought of walking past him to get to her creaky bed. Standing straight, and letting her shoulders slump, she tried walking through the room without making a sound.

"Ara, you smell like piss," her father said sharply, his eyes still on the newspaper.

She flinched. "Father—"

"Father?"

"Sorry. . . Tom." He had told her a few days ago not to call him father anymore. His need for control annoyed her, but she still complied. "I checked myself and I don't think—"

He glared at her. The muscles in his jaw tightened as he gritted his teeth.

"I. . ." she tried again, staring at the floorboards. "I will wash in the stream tomorrow morning." *Come on, let that be all.*

"Mr Mourey needs me to deliver an early shipment tomorrow," her father said as his eyes fell back to the partially ruined newspaper. "I need you to make it ready. The list is on the table."

Ara tightened her hands into fists. She would have to go to the marketplace before sunrise, make multiple trips back and forth with her small, broken wagon, *and* load the wares onto her father's large cart. Her exhausted muscles ached at the thought, and a word of protest threatened to leave her mouth.

"Your much-needed bath can't wait until tomorrow," he continued. "Do it now." He glared at her.

She met his eyes. He knew she wanted to oppose him, which would give him an excellent reason to release some pent-up aggression. His square jaw flexed. She needed all the sleep she could get before running to the marketplace for the items on the list and could bathe after her father left. There was no reason to be clean for a run to the market. Her mouth opened, her tongue about to form the words.

"If you do it now, you won't be wet while buying the wares," Nadia interjected to mediate the situation.

Ara looked out of the window, it was already dark, and the streets unsafe. He knew this.

"But—"

"Ara!" her father bellowed, standing. He was a tall man and he hovered menacingly over her. "You will do as I say and you will do it now!" He slapped her, now that she had given him a reason to, his elbow accidentally striking her mother's cup which toppled off the armrest, crashing to the floor.

Ara covered her reddening cheek, refusing to cry in front of him.

"Look what you made me do! Your disobedience shattered your mother's cup."

"It's fine," Nadia said quickly.

"Take the cup," her father commanded, sitting back in his chair. "She's seventeen now, it's time to learn her actions have consequences. Clean up your mess."

"My mess?" Ara frowned. "It was your—"

"Don't make me hit you again," he growled.

"Please, Ara," Nadia begged.

She begrudgingly picked up the pieces and put them on the table, before gathering the smaller pieces one-by-one into her hand.

"Use the broom," her father said.

Ara looked around the room, but it was nowhere. Her breathing quickened.

"You truly are hopeless. Your sister could have done it all without breaking anything," her father said. "If you'd only watched out for her."

Ara choked every time he mentioned her sister. "That's unfair—"

"If you'd protected her as any big sister should, she'd still be here with us. Instead, she's dead. The broom is outside."

Shaking with anger and sorrow, Ara opened the outside door, the cold wind finding its way through her thin clothes. He brought up her sister whenever he truly wanted to hurt her, knowing the sting of guilt was still as sharp as ever. The faint smell seeping around the house was stronger outside and dragged her from her trail of thoughts.

What is that?

The broom was propped against the wall of the wooden house. She grabbed it but hiding behind the brush was an iron snail that retracted.

Iron snails were helpful creatures. Their armour kept them safe from many predators, and they ate dangerous insects common in large cities, like heartflies. These nasty creatures were usually dealt with before winter when their eggs hatched, causing huge problems for the inhabitants of the Rundowns, which was a less sanitised area. They laid eggs inside people's mouths. The hatched larvae—thin, brown ghastly creatures— crawled down their throats, slowly eating away at their hearts.

As far as Ara knew, there was no cure, only preventative measures like a patch of cloth with two strings between the ears to keep them out. She carefully wiggled her hands under the iron snail's slimy body and it clung to her warm hand. She placed it under the long-since collapsed well and rearranged some of the bricks into a shelter for it.

"Ara!" her father bellowed from inside. "Close the door. You're letting out the heat!"

She sighed, grabbed the broom, and jogged back through the door, crashing into her father's chest.

"What is wrong with you today? Give me that." He snatched the broom from her hand. "I'll do it. Go bathe in the stream. If you don't come back smelling decent, you won't get to sleep in your bed."

He closed the door in her face.

She swallowed dryly to contain her anger. The quicker she did as asked, the better. Her district, the Rundowns, was especially unsafe at night. Kalastra was a beautiful city, but Ara lived in the most worn-down area.

It was only a ten-minute walk to the small stream, but it felt longer. Every individual she passed gave her uneasy stares—or that was how it felt. She didn't want them to see her marks from the beatings.

A pack of gnurgles following a man in dark robes approached her. Ara didn't know much about gnurgles, only that they imprinted on someone early in their lives, so the robed man was likely their master. The small, brown scaled creatures—about the size of a hand—had two tiny feet, large droopy ears, a pair of narrow black eyes, a thin mouth, and an overly large nose. Ara found them cute. They halted next to her feet, smelling her curiously before screeching and shying away, hurriedly returning to their master.

It wasn't long before Ara reached the stream at the very end of the Rundowns. Three guards patrolled close by. She pulled her hair in front of her face as stories of corrupt guardsmen having their way with young women flashed through her mind. Luckily, the stream was unlit, and the guards didn't see her sneak away from the road. She undressed and quickly washed. Still shaking from the cold water, she put her dirty, smelly clothes back on, and left the stream.

She hurried home, praying that her father would be asleep, but when she approached the house, sounds of fighting and shattering glass came from the open windows.

What's happening? Had father snapped?

Nadia screamed in agony. Ara stormed through the front door, stepping into a living nightmare. Her father was on the floor wrestling a giant six-legged beast. The beast's green scales shimmered in the dim light. With a short neck and a long head, its wide mouth glistened with sharp teeth, its long tail whipping around the room like a serpent. Sharp, menacing claws dug deep into the wooden floorboards.

The ceiling lantern swung violently, showing parts of the room in flashes. Her father was on his back, trying to fend off the creature. Ara saw blood, but not its source.

Where's Mother?

On the beast's back, faint wisps of black smoke emanated from two nostril-like holes. Her father slammed his fist into the beast's stomach, but it didn't seem to bother it. The monster was the size of a bull and looked just as strong. Neither her father nor the beast had noticed her.

Ara ran to the kitchen, crushing broken plates and glass underfoot. Grabbing a knife from the knife-rack, she darted back, stumbling over one of the toppled chairs, landing heavily on her arm. Pieces of broken wood, cutlery, and glass surrounded her. She felt warm liquid on her forearm, but the light was too dim for her to see clearly. Her father still wrestled the scaled beast a few feet away.

The creature had her father's arm in its mouth. He screamed in pain as the creature's teeth dug into his flesh, frantically punching its flat head with his other fist. Ara got up, struggling to keep her balance, and lunged toward it, attempting to stab the monster in its back. The knife didn't even penetrate its scales. She stabbed again and again, but nothing happened no matter where she tried, not even a scratch in the monster's natural armour.

The creature ripped her father's arm clean off, spraying blood everywhere. The sound was terrible, like thick taut strings tearing. The monster raised its head and gulped the limb down its throat, its claws digging into her father's legs, creating pools of blood on the floor.

Ara finally plunged the knife above its leg, digging into the tender flesh beneath the armour. The monster shrieked in pain as thick purple blood flowed from the wound. It shook its head in agony and scuttled away from her father, smoke gushing from the holes on its back, drowning the room in blackness.

The thick smoke made it hard to see and breathe, but Ara reached her father, coughing with the smoke filling her lungs, as the creature's tail slid over his thigh and disappeared. It was a few seconds before her father noticed her.

"Ara?" he said in wonder. "What are you doing here? We need to go!" He tried to grab her with his phantom arm and screamed.

She went around to her father's back and started dragging him away. The creature continued shrieking in pain somewhere within the smoke, thrashing about the room. Her father was heavy, so they moved slowly. Ara peeked at her forearm. There was blood, but it wasn't hers. Glancing over to the kitchen, the swinging lamp lit the area enough for her to see the source. Her mother was on the floor, her torso completely separated from her lower body. Her father fell as she let go and stumbled backwards, letting out a horrified scream.

"Ara," her father begged. "Help me!"

Was that Mother? It couldn't be. *She can't die.* The light flashed over the kitchen, showing a body split in half. "P— please, not. . ."

Her father grabbed her shirt and pulled her close. "She's dead, Ara."

The creature went silent—the room eerily still. The lantern's light wasn't strong enough to penetrate the thick blanket of smoke shielding the beast from sight. She peered into the darkness, trying to make out its ominous shape.

Like an eagle swooping down upon its prey, the creature leapt from the shadows. Its mouth sunk into her father's head, its serrated teeth digging into his neck. The beast shook its head violently and her father's skin began to tear, his hand waving wildly. With yet another violent tug, his neck ripped. Blood spurted, and Ara fell backwards, horrified, into a corner. The massive beast swallowed the head whole.

Her father's headless body slumped to the floor. The swinging lantern shone upon Ara and the beast shifted its focus. Yellow eyes peered directly at her. It crept slowly towards her, keeping low to the ground. Cornered, Ara pressed back against the wall, wishing the creature would just disappear. It readied itself for another lunge.

The door behind the creature blasted open and in stormed two men.

"We're not too late!" one exclaimed. It was hard to make out any details besides his long trench coat, dark skin, and large, round hat. "Quickly, get on it, Topper!"

Topper threw himself at the creature, landing on top of it. He was taller than the first man with the hat, but with a slimmer build and dark hair.

The beast twisted from side to side trying to shake off its attacker. It started climbing the wall, lifting Topper along with it.

"There we go," the man with the large hat said.

Ara sat completely dumbfounded, watching the events unfold before her.

The beast climbed onto a beam in the ceiling with Topper still clinging to it.

"Are you ready?" he screamed.

The man with the hat brought out something from a holster in his belt. "Ready!"

Topper poked his thumb into the creature's eye, making it screech and open its mouth. A loud bang followed, and Ara closed her eyes.

When she reopened them, the creature lay motionless on top of the man. His friend walked over and, with great effort, dragged the massive beast off him by the head.

Ara's hands shook, the contents of her stomach threatening to spill onto the bloody floor.

What just happened? Who were these men?

"Thank you," Topper said.

"Not gonna let you die today as well," the other one answered with a chuckle. He examined the creature. "Female, about eleven years old and yes. . . it's definitely a rura. You owe me a gold chip." He cast a smile at his companion who rose from the floor. "I know rura-piss when I smell it."

"Too bad we couldn't get here sooner," Topper said. "Might have been able to save them." The lantern light flashed over Ara, and he finally saw her. "Or maybe we actually *did* save someone. Khendric, come over here."

Khendric glanced at her. "Oh, by the craven's mother!" He rushed over and looked her up and down, narrowing his dark eyes. Then he surveyed the surroundings, locating her dead mother and the remains of her father. His frown deepened. "You poor, poor thing. I think you should come with us."

Come with them?

Ara couldn't piece together what had happened. Was the monster really dead, just like that?

"Poor girl," Topper said with an anxious look.

Ara's eyes darted from the dead beast on the floor, to her dead parents, and to the two men standing in her ruined living room. First she couldn't protect her sister, and now her parents. She really was useless.

Khendric looked at her, pity in his eyes. "It's going to be alright."

Her mind was blank. This didn't feel real. This couldn't be fixed. Never again would she hear her mother's voice, or peer into her warm eyes. In their last moment together, Ara pushed her away. "H—how," she began, her lips quivering, "will this be alright?"

Topper gave Khendric a blanket which he wrapped around her. "I don't know, but we'll help you."

CHAPTER 1

The Nature of Things

The light drizzle came to a stop. After riding on horseback for eight solid days, Ara's behind was sore. Her legs were the worst, and she was anxious to get off her horse and stretch. Her long hair was wet and plastered to her face. Her horse, Spotless, neighed and shook his head; he had many spots and was thus, not spotless at all.

Khendric took off his large, brown hat and brushed his hand over it as if that would somehow dry it. He ran his fingers through his black curly hair and gazed up towards the sky. Altogether, his strong cheekbones and jawline made him look determined.

"Finally, I thought the rain would never yield. Do you know where we are?"

Topper took in his surroundings. "I think we're only a day or so away from Cornstead."

Despite being in his early twenties, Topper often seemed boyish compared to Khendric, who Ara guessed was in his thirties.

"It's been quite some time since I was here last but as they say, 'the man who travels the world soon has the world in his pocket,'" Topper said. Khendric frowned. "That didn't work?"

"Well, it wasn't *too* bad. Surely better than 'a thief's aptitude is measured by his pocket change'. Or your worst one yet, 'the secrets of the past are always hidden in the future.'" Khendric laughed.

"I said that?" Topper blushed.

"You sure did. One of your many supremely wise sayings."

Ara smiled, trying to keep herself from chuckling.

"I need to remember that one," Topper said. "Because 'nothing keeps the mind as occupied as unwritten ideas'."

"And that's the last one for today," Khendric declared. "We haven't come this way in years. Are you certain we're close to Cornstead?"

"I've travelled this road more times than you in my many years," Topper said. "I have a great memory."

Many years? Ara wondered. *When you were a child?*

"And you remember that at exactly this spot, you were around a day away from Cornstead?" Khendric asked.

Topper scratched the back of his head. "It's more of a gut feeling, so more or less."

Topper's character was hard to pin down. Sometimes he talked as if he had been around for ages, other times he seemed as dim-witted as a child, struggling to lead a simple conversation with her. Not that Ara had been talkative—she spent most of her time in silence. What interesting conversation could a beaten-down seventeen-year-old girl offer? She'd make a fool of herself or bore them with her problems.

"Have you been this far away from home before?" Khendric asked her.

Ara shook her head. Khendric had seen where she lived so he must know she wasn't a traveller. Her father had also asked questions he already knew the answer to, questions that made her feel stupid, and she feared that Khendric was doing the same.

Ara had not told either of them about her past, how her parents had treated her, how her father had beaten her. She didn't dare. Khendric had taken her 'under his wing' as he put it, and for now, he treated her well. But so had her father for a long time, when times were good, and her sister Alena was alive. He blamed her death on Ara and had stopped considering her his daughter, but rather a reminder of what he lost that day. And he was right. It was Ara's fault. Alena's pure joy would light the darkest days in a way Ara never could, and because of her she was gone.

So Ara decided not to show weakness to the strangers. She hadn't even shed a tear for her mother. Instead, she locked her emotions deep inside.

Ara was more relieved to leave the city than she would admit, leaving the root of all her torment behind, even if it was with two strangers who'd stormed into her house one night. They had, after all, saved her.

Khendric rode closer. "So, what do you know about beast hunters?"

"You hunt beasts, right?"

"What gave it away?" He smirked. "Do you know what a rura is?"

Ara shook her head.

"We were working on another case when we passed your house. I smelled the urine of a beast known to live in swamps. After closing the case, we hurried to your house in hopes of dealing with the monster before it attacked."

"You knew it would attack?"

He nodded. "Ruras mark the places they intend to attack with urine, and we couldn't get back quickly enough."

"I smelled it," she said. "But I didn't know what it was."

"You couldn't have. They rarely enter urban territories."

I knew that smell wasn't me. She found comfort in knowing. *And the wind didn't blow the timber down, it was the rura.*

Grim thoughts of the beast surfaced. Ara didn't know how to feel—she had hated and loved her parents, but sometimes it felt great to be free and out in this new world. She had already seen so much more these past days than her whole life in the Rundowns—forests, pastures, creatures she had no idea existed. But then she would have moments where she felt guilty for her happiness. After all, she had lost her parents and had no family.

"Ara?" Khendric said. "I'm sorry if I've upset you. I thought maybe you'd like to know a bit more about how we found you."

She shot him a glance. *He almost looks sincere. Was he sorry he upset me? But why would he care?*

"I'm sorry," she said reflexively.

Khendric frowned. "Sorry about what? You've said or done nothing wrong." He clapped her on the shoulder causing her to flinch, but she tried to hide it. "So what do you think of the world? If you've only seen the walls of Kalastra, then you haven't seen much. What do you think about all of this around you?" He stretched out his arms.

"Umm," she began. "It's. . . very nice and a little exciting."

"Now, even that sentence is more cohesive than any of Topper's wise sayings." A smile spread across his face.

He smiles a lot, she thought. *Too much. He's planning something. He only brought me along for some devious plan*—the thoughts were stuck in her head. Her gut said they would betray her. But even with these thoughts, she couldn't convince herself to leave them. Where would she go? What would she do? She was nobody. So she stayed, with a glimmer of hope. Maybe her gut was, for once, wrong.

"I like these giant forests that surround the road," Khendric said. "One wouldn't know which creatures hide in there, and that's part of the excitement. Ara, have you ever seen so many trees in your life?"

She was astonished he found the uncertainty of unknown beasts in the forest exciting. "No, I've never seen this many trees."

"That's a shame," he said, shaking his head. "You've lived in a great city all your life, but never got to walk outside to actually explore the world and all its gifts."

"Mother said I could never go outside because of the beasts."

"Bah! Typical city-folk. You're all telling each other of the dangers outside the walls, but very few go outside to see for themselves. We've been on the road for days and so far, we've only seen a few narworms, browlers and a couple of treehowlers. Not much to be afraid of. Besides, there are just as many beasts inside the walls, as you would probably agree." He caught himself. "I'm sorry, sometimes I talk so much I forget what I'm saying."

She gave him a thin smile, and he looked away with a hint of embarrassment.

The sun rested on a mountain, its crimson light bathing their surroundings in soft light. Ara looked forward to reaching the village of Cornstead on the morrow, when, for a short time, her days wouldn't consist of sitting on horseback. The last sliver of sunlight was about to fade over the distant mountains, giving way to the coming night.

"Ara?" Khendric asked. "Can you check out that ledge?" He pointed a finger at what looked like a suitable campsite.

She reacted right away. "Yes."

"Don't do that."

"What?" she asked.

"Don't say 'yes' like that, as if I'm commanding you and you're answering out of fear of punishment. I can hear it in your voice."

"It won't happen again. I'm sorry."

"Ara." He chuckled lightly. "You're doing it again."

"I. . . hmm. . . I will check out that ledge?"

"Alright," he said with a hint of satisfaction. "You do that."

She steered Spotless off the dirt road towards the nearby ledge. The two men were talking, but she couldn't hear what they said.

He wanted me to go away so they could speak privately, she thought. *They didn't want me to hear.*

There was nothing to do about it, and they might be angry if she came back right away.

Stop it. Stop these thoughts.

The ledge seemed like a suitable place to sleep. They could set up camp under it, with the forest above them, though it wasn't ideal. Anything could crawl down from the trees, but it would soon be too dark to search for anywhere else.

She jumped off Spotless and took a pouch from the satchels at his side. She opened it, and the extreme odour hit her like a tidal wave. No matter how many nights she performed the safety procedures they had taught her, she never grew accustomed to the smell. She grabbed a handful of the powder from the pouch and strewed it around the prospective campsite. Nothing happened. She let out a relieved breath.

The acronal powder, or, as Khendric called it 'poop-powder' triggered spikers. Topper had told her of the small root-like creatures which grew from seeds deep in loose dirt, waiting for something to apply pressure to the surface above. With pressure, they shot up through the earth with terrifying speed, bursting forth with their venomous spike.

Spikers possessed a venomous neurotoxin, sufficient to immobilise a grown man, but potent enough to completely paralyse a child. The spiker would then survive on the blood from the wound it created, drinking until either the blood stopped, or the source was removed, at which point it quickly retracted into the earth.

Topper had shown Ara how to spread the poop-powder evenly, making the ground safe from the devilish creatures. The strong odour from the powder subdued spikers; they would stay that way until the next rainfall, or until the powder lost its scent.

After dispersing the poop-powder, she fetched the salt pouch from Spotless's other side. This pouch was running low, but she managed to create a circle around the perimeter. They hadn't told her why it was necessary. She wanted to ask but didn't want to burden them.

The next step was the sharp metal spikes. Pointy on both ends, she placed them in a circle too—twelve in total, to ward off duskdevils. She'd never seen one, but Khendric had told her they were shaped like a twisted human, crawling on all fours, their arms bent forward at an unnatural angle, and a twisted head with their mouths covering their noses. Lacking eyes, they used their sense of smell to track prey and were attracted by poop-powder—thus the metal spikes. The idea was these beasts would crawl into them, impaling themselves. Duskdevils couldn't jump, so the spikes proved an effective defence—or so Topper claimed.

When she finished setting up the spikes, the two men came over and dismounted, tying the animals to a piece of wood Topper stuck firmly in the ground. They removed their swords from their belts, and Khendric took off his coat and hat. His dagger, and an intricate rod-like device with a handle still hung around his waist, but Ara thought it best to dampen her curiosity and refrain from asking.

"No spikers?" Khendric asked, and Ara shook her head. "Any salt left then?"

"A little, but not enough for another night."

"Perfect," Khendric said. "Good job."

She frowned. *Good job? What's so good about it?*

Her father never complimented her on anything. She guessed it was to keep her wanting to impress him, which had worked. She'd constantly fought for a glimmer of his approval.

"Are you hungry?"

She was famished but dared not ask for food. She said nothing, but her eyes darted to the pouch with bread.

"That look tells me enough."

He. . . smiled?

Khendric dug into the bag, brought out a piece of bread, and offered it to her, and gratefully she took it. She had eaten well for the past two weeks, and it had done her a lot of good. Her malnourished frame was starting to fill out. She was growing strong and had a lot more energy.

"Khendric," Topper said, sitting across from Ara. "She ate that really fast."

She froze. Wasn't it hers to eat? Khendric chuckled and tossed her another piece of bread, bigger this time. She caught it, surprised.

"Let me know if you're still hungry after this one, alright?" he said.

She nodded. "Thank you."

"Ara," Topper said carefully. "Don't be afraid to tell us when you're hungry. As the old farmers say: Every man should remember—"

"What they were told earlier," Khendric interrupted. "You've already filled your day's quota on sayings."

"But this is a good one. Every man should remember what they've been told—isn't that what all ladies complain about?"

"Firstly, that's common sense, not some profound saying," Khendric said. "Secondly, yes, women do usually complain about men's forgetfulness. Although I've not personally had any problems with that."

"But of course not," Topper protested. "That would imply you've talked to a woman." He let out a bark of laughter.

"Ara's a woman!"

Topper's laughter caught in his throat, and he glanced nervously at her. "Of course, I never meant to imply that you... umm... weren't a woman. It's just—"

"Seems like beautiful young women make Topper go mute." Khendric laughed out loud as Topper reddened. "I didn't know you could turn *that* red!"

Ara's heart pounded. *I'm beautiful?* She'd never heard anyone speak about her like that. Her face grew warm.

"I will feed you to the varghauls!" Topper glared at him, which just made Khendric's grin even wider.

Ara couldn't stop her lips from curling into a small smile.

Khendric put his hat on. "Are you still hungry?"

A voice in the back of her head told her to say no. *Extra food means you owe him,* it whispered.

"No, thank you."

"I don't believe that for a second." Khendric handed her a satchel and when she opened it, she saw that it was filled with bread, fruit, and meat. "It's yours. Eat whenever you like."

Daring to trust his words, she immediately pulled out another piece of bread. Khendric nodded and rose to unsaddle his horse, opening an attached satchel. It always seemed like he tried hiding what he did next, and Ara had grown suspicious as the days passed. She shifted her focus from the food to Khendric. He faced the animal, conveniently blocking her vision as always. She tried to lean at different angles to get a better view, but to no avail.

Khendric fidgeted with his hands and put something inside the satchel. "I'll go check the forest quickly. You'll finish up here?"

Topper nodded in response.

Khendric glanced at Ara, the pupils of his eyes revealing a flickering, flaming glow. He turned away and climbed the ledge before disappearing into the woods. Ara stared at Topper, looking for some sort of explanation, but he still acted as if nothing was awry.

She'd first seen his eyes glowing a few days ago, and it had freaked her out then too, but Khendric and Topper always acted like nothing was wrong, so she tried to stay calm. Khendric was clearly trying to hide it though and as neither of them mentioned it, the secret was making Ara even more intrigued.

"Did you set up the nails?" Topper asked.

Without answering, Ara got up and retrieved them off of Spotless. The nails were woven together on a leather strip, which Ara placed in a circle around the small camp. They warded off some other little beasts, called rabdogs. Topper rose and cleaned the hooves of his horse while she set up the rest of the defensives.

Ara knew what rabdogs were—the streets of Kalastra were full of them. They hunted in small packs, scavenging for food and killing small prey like rats and other vermin. They kept the streets clean, but they also attacked children, sometimes even killing them, and then there was the real terror, a disease called rabness. Ara didn't know much about it, and she'd never seen anyone infected, but it was general knowledge that if a rabdog bit someone, they needed to find medicine from an infirmary quickly.

After placing the nails, she turned to Topper, who was still tending to his horse. There was a certain charm to his ragged hair—he didn't seem to care that it was in full chaos. He noticed Ara looking at him and nodded towards the other horses. She went to Spotless and gazed into his dark eyes.

Thoughts of her sister, Alena, surfaced in her mind again. She felt like she could hear the thundering hooves hammering on the pavement, her scream, and her trampled body. Ara was thirteen years old when Alena died. They were walking home alone through crowded streets, Alena clutching her simple, but precious doll. As they crossed a road, Ara realised she had lost hers and stopped. Alena noticed and came back to Ara. The street was full of people chattering and... that must have been why.

She didn't hear them, Ara told herself, recalling the horrible moment when the horses crashed into her.

After, everything changed at home. Her mother grew heartless. Her father became violent and uncaring, blaming her for Alena's death. *You didn't look after her*, he had screamed. Her hands shook as she pulled down the giant varghaul heads mounted on Spotless's back. She couldn't look into Spotless's eyes without remembering her guilt.

"Be careful with the trophies," Topper said.

She gripped the heads, or trophies as Topper called them, firmer. They stank of rotting flesh. The heads were horse-sized, but round instead of long. The wide mouths were full of sharp teeth with two larger fangs sticking out of the mouth like boar tusks. Ara could only speculate as to how Khendric and Topper had acquired the heads, especially since Topper told her they were flying beasts. The trophies alone struck fear into her heart. She mounted them on two spikes, facing them towards the sky.

"You're sure these will keep them away?" she asked. She hoped he didn't mind her asking, but her mind wandered— the words just slipped out.

"Oh, well, we're pretty sure," Topper said. "I've never heard of a varghaul diving to attack anyone using their heads like this."

"Do you know why?"

"We can't know for certain, but my guess is they don't attack someone who has already killed one of their kind."

"If I may ask," she said, curiosity getting the better of her, "how do you kill these things?"

"I don't know. I wasn't around when Khendric acquired these heads, but I think you have to shoot them down, or stab them as they dive towards you."

Now she was even more curious.

It must be an epic story, she thought, picturing Khendric in a heroic battle. *How could Khendric possibly kill two of these monsters alone?*

"But," Topper continued, "if one should happen to swerve across us and attack, the spears you're about to put up will come in handy."

She took the spears and plunged them into the ground, tips up.

"Besides, varghauls probably won't attack someone as smelly as Khendric." He laughed lightly.

Ara didn't even realise it was a joke until it became awkward and they just exchanged embarrassed glances and she continued her work.

CHAPTER 2
The Red Book

At last, the camp was fully set up. It was such a hassle, but Khendric said, "The quicker you learn, the longer you live."

Ara sat on a stone close to the ledge while Topper kindled the fire. It barely lit their small campsite, and the nearby road was soon swallowed by the coming night. The wind rustled the trees around them, almost hiding the moon from sight. She pulled out another piece of bread and wondered whether Topper would approve, but he didn't react, so she ate until she wasn't hungry.

Footsteps approached from above the ledge. Her eyes darted back and forth for signs of life, but it was only Khendric coming back from whatever he had been doing. Ara immediately looked at his eyes, expecting to see the flaming amber glow, but they were normal. It left her a bit dissatisfied.

The flaming eyes must help him see in the dark, she thought, but how he got them remained a mystery.

"I see the camp is set up properly," he said with a grin. "Nice, Ara."

Once again, she didn't know how to react to compliments. He entered the camp, avoiding the spikes and nails and passing the horses, and sat down beside Topper on a tree stump.

"So? Anything?" Topper asked.

"You may sleep without fear of monsters tonight, my dear Topper."

"I'm not scared," Topper proclaimed, shooting a glance at Ara. "It's just nice to know."

It made her more comfortable to know there weren't any beasts around. Her eyes drifted to the varghaul heads, and she dreaded the thought of ever meeting such a winged terror. Becoming painfully aware of her unprotected back to the darkness beyond the campfire, she turned around. Still, she saw nothing.

"Don't worry," Khendric said with a comforting voice. "There's nothing out there. At least not right now."

Ara looked at his warm eyes.

Nothing escapes you, Khendric, she thought.

Staring into those eyes, a sense of safety sparked inside her, a feeling she hadn't had for a very long time.

"How did you get those heads?" she asked.

Khendric turned to the trophies. "I bought them," he said nonchalantly.

"Oh," Ara replied, dumbfounded.

Topper frowned.

"What?" Khendric said. "Varghauls are rare! I've only seen one in my thirty-two years. But in case one would chance over us, we're safe."

She sighed in mild disappointment, her image of a heroic battle shattered.

"I didn't know you thought so highly of me, Ara," Khendric said, causing her to blush—she stared hard at the ground. "I'm a bit too old for you, I'm afraid." He raised a cup of water to his lips.

That made her turn even redder.

"Khendric," Topper said. "You're not an ugly guy, but *this* is like watching a stone flirt with a princess."

Khendric spat out the water he was drinking. "Topper! You're the last person I expect to throw such comebacks. Well done, you snivelling stonepudder!"

"Not to mention, you're practically ancient compared to her," Topper added.

"Alright, alright, an old soul can only take so much of a beating. That brings up a good point, though. Have you heard of narworms?" Ara shook her head. "They're small larvae beasts, about the same size as rabdogs. Thick and brown."

"I detest them," Topper added.

"Most do. They aren't that dangerous now and certainly not to Topper or me, but they're nicknamed child-eaters, because these wormy creatures slowly crawl towards unsuspecting children. When they're within two feet, they take an awkward leap at the child. With their suction mouth, they attach themselves to an arm or a foot. By that point, they're hard to remove from the poor child, and the worm starts to suck, moving slowly up the captured body part. I've heard their spit contains digestive juices, so the poor victim can feel their limbs slowly being digested. Dreadful way to go, I'd say, excruciatingly painful."

Ara's eyes grew wide in horror.

"They only attack children as they're small themselves," he continued. "They track them by their scent. The oldest person I've heard of being attacked by a narworm was fifteen. How old are you?"

"Seventeen!" she exclaimed without hesitation.

"You're safe then," Khendric said. "Even though you're pretty small, you don't secrete the correct pheromones they pick up on."

Ara felt her nerves ease and her stomach unclench.

Khendric dug around in a satchel. "Here." He handed her a thick, clearly well-read book. "In it you'll find a description of every beast I know. It would be good for you to know about as many as you can, in case you ever encounter one of them."

It was a beautiful, dark-red book with a smooth leather cover. Ara wanted to hold it but when her father gave her something, he asked twice in return later. He'd never given her something as intriguing as a book, which meant the price to pay for this would be dear.

"Go on, take it." He pushed it towards her.

"It's a good book," Topper added.

But she didn't move.

Khendric grabbed her satchel and put the book in it, nonetheless. "I want you to read about one beast a day. Reading on horseback is not ideal, but you'll get used to it." Ara sat still, not reacting to his words. "I'm sorry to push it on you, but it really could save your life someday."

"Can you read?" Topper asked gently.

She nodded. She was itching to read it; she'd never had a book of her own. Her mother taught her to read from sheets, but they never had a real book in the house. She didn't want to seem too eager because that would only create a larger debt.

Four clunking noises in the tree above her sounded out from the rustling leaves. She sprang to her feet, skipped over the fire, and landed between Khendric and Topper.

"I—I heard something!" She pointed to the tree. "Like something moved up there."

The beast hunters rose, and Khendric cautiously walked closer while Topper stayed by her side. As Khendric neared, the clunking noises came again, sounding like wood against wood.

"It's just a barkskin," he said. "I can make out its shape in the moonlight."

"Was it going to eat me?" Ara asked, eyes wide.

"No, it just wants to put out our fire." Khendric broke off a branch and came back, taking Ara's stone to sit on. He broke off some twigs and held it over the flames.

Ara sat on his tree stump, keeping her eyes on the tree. "Put out our fire?"

"They're a large insect, about the size of your forearm, but instead of a hard carapace, their skin is bark."

She looked at her forearm, imagining it crawling just above her head, causing shivers down her spine.

"It's completely harmless," Khendric continued as his branch caught fire. "But to be sure it is a barkskin, here's how you test it." He tossed the burning branch past the tree. The clunking returned, rapidly this time, scaling down the tree.

Ara rose from the stump just in time to spot a six-legged, bark-skinned creature with a rectangle-shaped body digging and tossing dirt at the burning branch, putting out the fire.

"Now we know for sure," Khendric said.

The clunking returned, the barkskin climbing back into its tree.

"It won't do anything until we go to sleep," Topper said. "And now we know we won't start a forest fire."

"Because it will crawl down and put out our fire?" Ara asked.

"Exactly," Khendric said.

Khendric and Topper lay down on the bare ground, looking at the night sky, seeming to have forgotten about the barkskin already. They looked so comfortable—sleeping out in the wild, under the stars.

Khendric narrowed his eyes before propping himself up on his elbows. "No way," he said in wonder, almost in awe. "Topper, is that a—"

"Pharlanax?"

Ara gazed at the night sky. Far, far above, a strange light twinkled. Instead of pale, white starlight, an orange glow drifted across the sky. It was tiny, not much bigger than the stars themselves, and it flickered, leaving a trail behind it.

"I can't believe this. If you can picture it, Ara, it's a giant burning bird."

Ara frowned. "A burning bird?"

"It's constantly burning with a weird concoction of molten lava, shadow, and smoke. It's hard to explain. I've only seen drawings, and they depict it as if shadow has taken form, churning around the beast together with lava," Khendric explained.

Ara tried to picture the bird in her head. She looked up again and thought maybe she could see wings flapping, despite it being a tiny dot in the sky.

"This is an incredibly rare occurrence." Khendric smiled at her. "Only with us for two weeks and now we see a pharlanax! You're lucky."

It traversed the sky, leaving a mesmerising fiery line behind it. She imagined being up there, seeing the world from above. How free it must feel, soaring through the night, going wherever it wished.

"Wow," she uttered, following it with her eyes. "Why is it so rare?"

"Firstly, there are only a few of them, and we don't know how they reproduce. There are theories. Some claim they're born from the ashes of disasters, like a village burned to the ground. Some say they're the remnants of a divinity that lived long ago, but that sounds more like a children's story. It's a good thing they're rare though, because they're incredibly dangerous. They attack unprovoked. You see that faint line of light behind the beast?" He pointed towards the sky. Ara nodded. "That's molten lava constantly emanating from it, creating the trail you can vaguely see. That high up it's not dangerous, as the fire cools before doing any damage, but if it flies low above a forest, the lava can create great forest fires. Or if it attacks a village or a city, basically everything will burn. Wherever it goes, only ashes remain."

Soon the bird was out of sight, disappearing behind the mountains far to the east.

"There's a lot of mysticism surrounding those birds. Their ashes are immensely valuable, as with them you can easily kill wretchers. People have also claimed to gain extraordinary powers from ingesting the ashes, but those are just stories, I figure." He lay back down on the ground. "I think there's a lot we do not know about these majestic creatures, but one thing is for sure: we're safe from varghauls for the night. Pharlanaxes hunt them, and it always ends badly for the varghaul."

Ara shot a glance at the enormous varghaul heads.

That bird kills those things?

She looked to the sky once more, making sure it was gone.

* * *

Khendric and Topper were fast asleep but Ara wasn't tired at all. Despite not knowing them well, sitting out in the firelight felt safer than being home in Kalastra with her parents. She watched them, wondering how these men were so unlike her father. Every time she began to draw links between the three men, they instead contradicted in every way. Even in giving her the book, it seemed as though Khendric intended no harm. Perhaps there would be no future debt, which was a dangerous thought if she was wrong.

As the fire crackled, she considered what an unexpected turn her life had taken. She would have been dead had it not been for the two hunters storming into her parents' house.

Now she was sitting here, under the stars, surrounded by traps to ward off various creatures and so far away from what she had once called home. Her thoughts drifted and before long she fell asleep.

CHAPTER 3

The Beasts of Cornstead

As the first shred of light grazed the mountains in the distance, Ara's eyes opened. She had fallen asleep sitting upright, and her lower back ached. Khendric and Topper were still sleeping on the ground.

With tired eyes, she scouted the area. All looked as it should. She'd dreamt of the rura—the lizard beast—her dreams mostly a replay of what had happened with small variations. She was getting used to the nightmares, as terrible as they were. Like everything in her old life, they were familiar and painful.

With the darkness of night vanishing quickly, it should be safe to dismantle the camp's defences, now a simple routine. The trophies were removed first, followed by the spears, the nails, and the metal spikes. Ara counted eleven. There was just a hole where the twelfth should have been. She looked closer, seeing a dark yellow goo.

"Khendric?"

He struggled to open his eyes. "What?" he mumbled.

"We're missing a spike!" she said frantically, pointing to where she'd thrust it into the ground last night. Topper was up, already examining the area. "I saw some yellow goo!" Ara added.

He inspected the small crime scene, smelled the goo, and turned around. "It was a dustdevil. This is dustdevil blood, and it probably ran off as soon as it was impaled, carrying the spike with it." He went to gather up his things.

"That's it?" Ara asked. There had been a *beast* crawling up on them at night, probably wanting to kill her, without her even noticing. She shivered just thinking about it.

"We're lucky to be alive," Khendric said with a sarcastic smile.

Ara closed her mouth, meeting him with a blank stare. "What if it had attacked?"

"Then I'd have killed it," Topper said. But Ara wasn't satisfied. "Quickly?" he added.

Ara crossed her arms, scouting the camp for signs of the thing.

"Oh, don't worry," Khendric said, putting on his hat. "Dustdevils are squeamish beasts. A pistol shot would probably have scared it off."

A what-shot? Ara wondered.

"They're not too unusual," Topper said. "Dustdevils exist in all kingdoms, and metal spikes have proved to be sufficient defence against them."

"Did we lose the spike?" Khendric asked. She nodded. "Too bad. You were never in any real danger," he said, noticing her stiff stance. "If the spike hadn't got it, we'd have killed it before it had a chance to attack. And they always travel alone. Once it was dead, we would have been safe for the rest of the night."

It didn't settle Ara's stomach, but there was nothing else to do other than pack. They readied the horses, and before long were on their way.

"We should reach Cornstead sometime after noon," Topper said, pushing his horse to a trot.

"You should start reading, young miss," Khendric said to Ara.

The book was in her hands in seconds. She'd been thinking about it since she climbed back onto Spotless.

"Maybe we'll find our culprit lying dead in our path as well," Khendric said. "And get our spike back. Never knew a dustdevil to be a thief."

"Was that a joke?" Topper asked.

"A poor attempt at one."

Topper was smiling though, and Ara offered a forced one. Khendric chuckled and pointed her down into the book. The first page read:

Mimeits

Known location: Kingdom of Paradrax and scattered reports of attacks in the neighbouring kingdom of Bodera, the Mud-Lands.

Type: Parasitic

Weakness: Fire, acid and general weaponry

Mimeits are insectoid beasts about the size of a man's forearm. Their heads have random spiked patterns and four eyes arranged in a similarly arbitrary manner. Their leg-count varies from six to twelve. Their eggs will only hatch inside a host body, such as pigs, cows, or humans.

Mimeits drop eggs inside said individual's mouth. A mimeit will usually drop somewhere between ten to forty eggs.

The nature of the eggs is quite peculiar, and about one fifth of them grows to be new mimeits. The other eggs, however, seem to mimic different organs or features of the host, displaying them in awkward places on the body. The host will often die of secondary infections unless a vital organ is mutated to such degree that it shuts down.

Example: *Prisoner in Teria, Paradrax. The female prisoner was sentenced to death for unknown crimes, and it was not known mimeits had infected her. She was left in isolation. With no way to commit suicide, the parasitic eggs grew unimpeded. She was found dead on the day of her execution. In the room were eight mimeits, so I believe the mother-mimeit dropped approximately forty eggs into the woman's stomach. A list of the growths follows:*

External lesions:

- Five new eyes in various locations on the body.

- Four toes, all on the right side of the neck.

- A second, well-developed, mouth on the left cheek.

- Four new teeth on the skull.

- A small arm from under the right armpit.

Internal lesions:

- An abnormal lobe of lung tissue on the pre-existing right lung.

- A second liver attached to the stomach. It should be noted that one of the mimeits escaped the room, and

after a week, many prisoners displayed symptoms of infestation.

To prevent further spreading, the prison was burned to the ground, with all prisoners inside. Though brutal, it proved very effective.

- Alec

Ara didn't know how to react. She was disgusted by the thought of being infected, but at the same time, it was interesting to read. She grimaced.

"She just read about the mimeits," Khendric said to Topper, his tone cheerful. "Those little bastards might be the worst thing to ever happen to this world. People affected are often referred to as abominations and with good reason." He shuddered.

"You look like you've met your fair share of mimeits in your life, Khendric," Topper said. "That nose couldn't have occurred naturally, and that double chin. . ."

Khendric chuckled, and Ara stifled a laugh.

She glanced back towards their campsite, which was no longer within eyesight. "I have a question about the mimeits. If they grow different body parts, can they be used to grow new limbs for people who have, for example, lost a leg?"

Khendric considered her words. "I have heard it's been tried. But I also heard it had disastrous results. A good question, though."

It pleased her to hear him say that, but she tried not to show it. Showing too much emotion was not something she did around strangers. But were they truly strangers anymore? She felt like she knew them better than she had ever known her parents. It was a conflicting thought. They'd been nothing but kind to her since rescuing her from the rura, providing her with food and protection, but could she trust them?

She turned the page; the next entry was about something called morgals.

"Are morgals as nasty as mimeits?" she asked. "Cause my stomach—"

Khendric's dexterous hand flipped to the next page. "Yes, way worse. I would skip those. They're rare, boring, and irrelevant."

"Sorry," Ara said.

"Don't apologise," he said warmly, and carefully closed the book. "Plus, we're getting close to Cornstead."

Smoke rose behind a nearby hill, revealing the faint and familiar sounds of a village. After riding horseback for so long, she was excited. Despite her shyness, seeing faces other than Khendric's and Topper's would be a welcome change.

Cornstead was a lot bigger than Ara expected. The village was surrounded by a wooden fence that ran up a hillside and through a forest. Kalastra was an enormous city, so Ara had naturally assumed the town would consist of only a few houses, some orchards, a butcher's shop, and maybe a smithy. But this was more like a small city, probably housing a few thousand people.

They approached the main gate, where a soldier stood guard, sword resting on his shoulder. Ara tightened her jaw, growing nervous in front of the guard.

"Visitors or residents?" he asked. The soldier held his chin high and puffed out his chest to the point of bursting.

"Visitors," Khendric answered. "But it's not the first—"

"Are you planning to stay overnight?" the soldier interrupted.

"Yes, at the—"

"Then you may take your horses through the gate for one silver chip each. If not, you may place them outside of the village walls until you leave."

There was a moment of silence, then Khendric smiled. "That breastplate of yours seems a bit too big for you. Did you acquire it only a short time ago?"

"Why would you care? Now it's one silver chip for—"

"Yes," Khendric interrupted. "You've already told us of your horse-entry payment. However, I think you might be in the wrong kingdom. The latest news from Kalastra, the capital, regarding guard duties, states that constables will handle such affairs, but that's not where you went wrong, my dear man. The sword you are so elegantly displaying has the Sangerian Grasslands emblem branded on it, and the greenish hue of that breastplate matches the official colour of the Sangerian's armour exactly. So your jurisdiction here is somewhat debatable."

The soldier's hands fidgeted; his feet shuffled.

Ara couldn't believe how the paradigm had changed simply from Khendric's words. Her nervousness turned to anticipation.

"But those are only the obvious faults in your 'guard duty' here. There are drops of blood on your left gauntlet and under your left ear. You have also been favouring your left leg. Even since you began to shuffle, you've kept your weight off your right foot. The Sangerian sword you bear does not match your empty sheath. And if I'm being critical, your boots are incredibly muddy for one who's been standing guard. I guess you're a murderer and a thief. You most likely killed a Sangerian patrol with your accomplices, took their armour and sword, travelled all the way to Cornstead, and here you stand, pathetically asking visitors for silver chips as they bring their horses into the village! How on earth did you get this brilliant idea? Must have taken all your brainpower."

A bead of sweat ran down the soldier's forehead. He swallowed dryly.

"So, here is what we're gonna do," continued Khendric. "And only because I'm in a good mood today. You're gonna lay the sword down and remove your breastplate, then you'll walk away and never return to Cornstead. Alternatively, you don't do that and I shoot you dead right here and now." Ara heard a click, and Khendric aimed the weird-looking rod-like device at the soldier.

"Shoot me?" the perpetrator asked with a trembling voice. "What is that in your hand?"

"This is a pistol. It's fairly new to the market. With it I can fire a small iron ball so fast it would penetrate your head, leaving your brain splattered all over the pretty wall behind you."

The man dared not move, staring at the device with uncertain eyes. "That little thing can do all that?"

"Do you care to find out?" Khendric asked.

The man slowly put his sword down and awkwardly removed his breastplate. He backed away from the village, not even bothering to look over his shoulder.

"Aren't you going to thank the man who let you live?" Topper shouted.

"Umm, yes, yes—thank you, my lord," the man said, scampering away.

Khendric chuckled and slid his pistol back into his belt.

"Did you hear that?" Khendric said. "'My lord.'" He laughed.

Ara's mouth dropped open—she quickly shut it. "How did you know all that?"

Khendric shrugged. "Well, it was simple; I just looked at him. When you know where to look and what to look for, it's not too difficult. Maybe I can teach you."

Now *that* was something she wanted to learn. Just from what Khendric had observed, he had disarmed the man, making him powerless.

He winked at her as they entered the village. After passing through the gate, they entered a marketplace filled with people. Children ran in the streets playing and singing; men haggled, and the general chatter gave Cornstead a lovely charm. From their carts, merchants presented wares of all sorts, from food to clothes, to pocket watches, and even some weaponry. After passing through the market, they dismounted and tied their horses to poles outside an inn called The Grindstone.

"Ara, you go with Topper and buy some salt, bread, and any other food you might like."

Topper immediately blushed. "Maybe you two can do that. Besides, I hate haggling."

"Oh, nonsense." Khendric smirked. "Now is a good time for you to get to know each other better."

"Where are you going?" Ara asked as Khendric started up the steps to the inn.

"I'm going to rent two rooms for a night or two and carry our supplies inside. Starting with those two, or someone will steal them." He pointed at the varghaul heads, tipped his hat, and disappeared inside.

Ara turned—Topper was already on his way to the market.

She caught up just as he approached a merchant.

"Do you have salt?" he asked the man behind the cart.

The merchant's hair was dark, thin, and dry, hanging down to his shoulders. He had a big nose, thick eyebrows, and a rat-like face.

A manris rested on his shoulder—a furry creature with six legs and two heads. Some merchants owned them due to their natural ability to change fur colours before rainfall, alerting them to move their exposed wares under cover. It slept soundly, still holding on tight to the merchant's clothing. Ara had seen them many times before and knew its orange colour meant no rain would fall for a while.

"I have salt," he said brusquely. "How much you need?"

"I'll take four ounces," Topper said, getting his pouch.

Opening it, Ara's eyes widened at seeing a golden chip among four silver ones. She had only ever had six silver chips—a golden one was worth twenty. It seemed that Ara wasn't the only one peeping; the merchant cast a quick glance into Topper's pouch.

She knew showing your chips to a merchant early gave him a chance to spot how much you had, allowing him to ask for more money. The merchant turned around and began weighing some salt.

Is this some clever ploy? she wondered, looking at Topper with anticipation.

The merchant turned back and presented a small pouch with salt. "One gold chip," he said casually.

At first, Topper seemed perplexed, but handed him exactly that amount.

Ara was dumbfounded, she couldn't believe the massive fortune Topper was about to give away.

That salt is worth no more than one silver chip.

Her whole life she had been going to market, buying supplies for her father's transport business. She could easily discern a good deal from a terrible one.

"Stop! Weigh the pouch again."

The merchant frowned at her. "Pardon me, are you suggesting that I cheat? Do you always let your lady interrupt your business?" he asked Topper.

Ara leaned close to Topper. She didn't care what the merchant thought. Growing up in this environment, she was used to haggling. "He's trying to undermine me," she whispered. "This means he's hiding something. You're paying way more than what this salt is worth."

"I don't know what you think you know about salt," the merchant said to Ara, snatching back Topper's attention, "but around here it's not easy to come by. Makes it more valuable, hence the price." He crossed his arms, looking away.

Please, Ara thought, waiting nervously for Topper to say something. *Listen to me.*

Topper looked the merchant in the eye. "Do it," he said, handing the pouch back.

The merchant hesitated but, looking into Topper's unyielding face, he did as asked. The scale put the weight at three ounces only, instead of four. "I. . . must have made a mistake."

"Hmm," Topper hummed. "That is quite strange. Maybe the village authorities would like to know about this?"

"Now, now," the merchant said. "It would simply be your word against mine."

"I'm a witness," Ara said. "I'll say I also heard four ounces."

The merchant gritted his teeth.

"It doesn't matter." Topper shrugged. "My father is the captain of the constables overseeing this village, one word to him and no one will care what you have to say. First, you lie about the price, then you have the nerve to lie about the weight. You're a common thief, and I could have you hanged—"

"I'm sorry. . . please!" the merchant pleaded, falling for Topper's lie, his defiance melting away. "I have a family and—"

"One more lie, and I'll cut out your tongue and make you eat it." Topper brought out his dagger, slamming it into the wooden table.

"Alright," the merchant said. "The salt is free of charge."

"That is the least you can do," Topper said, taking the pouch. "I'm taking some bread and mutton chops, also free of charge."

The merchant ground his teeth. "Fine. Take it."

They left the merchant with more wares than planned.

"Well done, Ara!"

"Thank you," she said, actually producing a little smile. "I didn't realise my market experience would come in handy."

"Well, it certainly did. I only had one gold and four silver chips left, so you saved me a fortune."

She felt better than she had in a long time, a sense of self-worth sparking to life.

CHAPTER 4
The Old Man's Mystery

The duo roamed the market for the supplies they needed, with Ara at the helm. Topper named the wares, and she obtained the best deal possible. She couldn't wait for Khendric to hear of how helpful she'd been.

The last thing they needed was acronal powder. Topper lead her into an alley that branched out from the marketplace. They reached a thin door with dusty windows and a faded sign that read Beast Hunter Store.

Inside the tiny shop, a round man was seated behind a counter. The interior was old, but cosy, with shelves of mysterious souvenirs, like oddly-shaped nails, fangs, stubs of hair, even some small daggers. Despite wanting to browse, Ara stayed behind Topper. Behind the merchant was a padlocked door.

"What can I interest you in today?" the merchant asked, grinning from ear to ear.

"I am a beast hunter," Topper said, handing a medallion to the man.

"I see." The merchant studied it briefly, handed it back, and unlocked the door behind him.

Heart full of anticipation, Ara followed Topper through the door. The merchant closed it behind them.

"If anyone asks, say you're a beast hunter," Topper whispered to Ara as they walked along a dark hallway.

"What? But I'm not!"

"Don't worry, there will probably only be one old man in here, and I'll do the talking."

"I can't lie." Her hands started to tremble. "I'll just go back."

"No, the merchant will know something's up. Just stay quiet, it'll be fine." He grabbed her shoulders with both hands. "Trust me."

Her stomach tightened into twisted knots. Ara had trouble with those two words.

They entered a cramped, barely-lit shop, with shelves upon shelves crammed with items. Four slender wooden pillars were set in a square formation in the centre of the room, surrounded by round tables displaying jars of dirt, various body parts which Ara could only guess were from different beasts, and many other objects like teeth, hairballs, tiny brains, and powders. Grey smoke swirled in the air.

"What is it you seek, beast hunters?" a cranky voice asked.

Behind the counter, sat a diminutive old woman, holding a pipe. She had a round wrinkled face, her eyes barely open, and she wore large wooden piercings in her nose, lips, and ears.

Ara tried to merge with the shadows, avoiding the woman's attention.

"We need acronal powder," Topper said.

"Ah, poop powder. I'll prepare it. You may browse our other wares in the meantime." She hopped off her chair and disappeared behind a curtain.

Ara's curiosity sparked as she inspected the merchandise. "What's this?" she asked, pointing to a bunch of dried-up, purple fingers, with nails like talons.

"I think they're mildwever fingers," he said, picking one up. "They tend to rot crops. Nasty little buggers."

"And this?" She held a small, jade-green clam.

"That is an antitoxin clam. It will remove any toxin from—"

"And this?" This place was so cool, and she wanted to know about every single thing in here.

"Umm, that is a wretcher's talon, for killing scrumts."

It was long enough to pierce right through her body.

Beside it, in a brown pot, stood a beautiful green and purple flower with blue leaves, its leaves and petals gracefully twirling in the air. Ara carefully let it run over her hand—a small animal face dug itself up from the dirt, watching her with four green eyes.

"Topper?" she said, getting his attention.

The creature dug itself out of the pot, revealing its pink wriggly skin and four fangs. It was no bigger than her forearm, but it scared her enough to take three steps back.

"Don't worry," Topper said. "It's just a rapler. Completely harmless."

The beautiful flower she'd touched appeared to be its tail. The rapler jumped down from the pot, shook off the rest of the dirt, and walked through the room to another pot where it dug itself down.

"Did I do something wrong?"

"No, you just annoyed it so it changed places. When leaves fall from their tail, they somehow turn them into a rare and exquisite tea which is sold all over the world, I think."

"Really?"

"Yeah, I've tasted it once, and it's fantastic. If someone offers you mill-tea, you drink it. Having that single rapler here probably brings in a lot of gold chips."

"Thanks, I'll remember." She was about to pick up a new item when the little old lady returned.

"That's an awful lot of questions for a beast hunter," she said, seating herself back on the chair.

Ara's pulse quickened. *She knows.*

"She's quite new," Topper said quickly.

"How refreshing!" she exclaimed and smiled warmly. Ara sighed, relieved. "It's been a while since I saw a female beast hunter in training."

"Yes, she's a natural. Managed to wound a rura without any training."

"And who are you?" she asked, pointing at him with a long pipe before putting it between her lips. It lit without her doing a thing.

"Oh, I am Tornas. I'm with Khendric." Ara didn't know why he used a fake name, but she held her tongue.

The old woman's grin reappeared. "Khendric's apprentice or apprentices. I've never met him myself, but I have heard of him. Be careful with that man. If I remember correctly, over the last few years he's changed pupils frequently. I'm not judging, merely pointing out that nobody knows what happened to them all."

Topper scratched his neck. "Yeah, anyway, did you get the powder?"

"Oh, yes," she said, placing a small pouch on the counter. "Do you need anything else?"

Topper grabbed the pouch and gave her three silver chips as payment. "No. That's all."

"Wait," Ara blurted out. All eyes fell on her. "We... need a spike."

He snapped his fingers. "Right, I almost forgot."

"Trouble with dustdevils, I see," the old woman said, puffing out a cloud of smoke. "I hate those wretched beasts." She went and found a spike which Topper bought.

There was so much more Ara wanted to know about all the mysterious items in the room, but Topper signalled for them to leave. As they left, Topper handed a silver chip to the merchant. From the merchant's sleeve crawled two gnurgles, sniffing the small piece of metal. They licked it frantically, and the merchant seemed pleased.

"I thank you," he said.

"What did those gnurgles do?" Ara asked as they walked back to the marketplace.

"Many merchants use them to spot counterfeit gold. The gnurgles can smell the difference with their large noses."

Sudden realisation dawned upon her.

That's why the gnurgles were scared of me the day of the rura-attack, they smelled the rura urine.

"Listen, Ara. That place is only for beast hunters." He ruffled his dark hair. "So just keep it a secret."

She nodded, feeling privileged to know such a place existed.

The marketplace was still crowded with people, and Ara trailed behind Topper. The crowd lightened as they entered a broad street. She had one question she was dying to ask but wasn't sure if it was appropriate until her curiosity got the better of her. "Topper?"

"Yes?"

"Why did you lie about your name?"

Topper's eyes shifted frantically before he looked away. "Err. . ."

Ara regretted asking and knew she had crossed a line. Her heart raced inside her chest. "I'm so sorry for asking."

"No, it's fine. It's just. . . a bit personal. But that was a natural question, of course." He looked at her, seeming to pick up on her anxiety. "Maybe I'll tell you sometime."

They met Khendric at the entrance to the inn and he showed them to the room he had rented. It was gorgeous with a large bed, clean windows, a chair, and even a mirror.

"Ara, here's the key to your room," Khendric said.

Frowning, she asked, "My room?"

"Right next door. I think it's best for you to have your own."

Her mouth dropped. *My own room?* "That must have been too expensive."

"Don't worry about it," he said easily.

"You probably saved us that amount at the market today," Topper said. Khendric furrowed his brows questioningly. "You should have seen her! She bartered and haggled, saving me a lot of chips."

"Really?" Khendric said, a huge grin on his face. "I'm impressed."

She beamed with happiness, standing taller than ever.

"Seems you've earned that room. Now go have some well-deserved alone-time."

She opened the magnificent door to a room of equal size. Khendric had put a new set of clothes on the massive bed—blue breeches and a white linen shirt. She'd never owned new clothes and she changed rapidly before twirling in front of the mirror. Her head buzzed with emotion, and she fell onto the bed, exhaling heavily. It felt good to be finally alone.

Khendric had offered to buy her and Topper a few drinks that evening. Ara had never tried alcohol and was intrigued to know what it tasted like. They went to a bar called the Happy Haggler. Nearly every table was populated with an assortment of people, and the bar was lively with chatter and laughter.

"Did you find the room to your liking?" Topper asked once they sat down.

"Yes it's lovely and thank you for the clothes but I don't want you to spend any more chips on me."

Khendric frowned. "Oh, do you feel guilty?"

She nodded.

"Ara, you have nothing. I have a little more. Don't worry, I didn't spend enough to put Topper and I at any risk.

After what happened to you, we want to help you get back on your feet again."

"But, why?"

"Because if we hadn't been working another case, we might've saved your family."

"You don't owe me anything," Ara said, staring at the table. "You saved my life."

His grin returned. "It's not only guilt. I think you're a good person and we've grown to like you."

She chuckled softly, unsure how to react to such kind words.

Topper set a mug in front of her. She leaned back, nervous. "It's a sweet wine," he said.

"Have you ever tasted wine before?" Khendric asked.

She shook her head.

"Try a sip."

She nodded and raised the mug to her mouth. They both stared at her expectantly. It tasted sour and bitter at the same time, but she managed to keep a straight face.

"So?" they both asked.

"It's. . . not that good," she answered.

"I told you!" Khendric said, slapping Topper's shoulder. "Pay up, gnurgle!"

Topper dug into his pockets with a sour expression. "Fine. A chip given today, will turn into a favour on the morrow."

Khendric laughed. "You're like a failed singer that refuses to leave the stage."

Topper tilted his head and sighed. Even Ara had to laugh.

Once the laughter died, Khendric leaned closer. "Until now, your path since we rescued you has been unclear." Her eyes grew wide, her smile fading, as worry twisted in her guts. "I've been thinking about it and we've decided to travel to Ashbourn, the capital of the Sangerian Grasslands. I've been before, and the city is wonderful. I know a lovely woman who's in charge of an infirmary, and I'm hoping she can hire and train you to be a nurse." He looked at her with his arms out. "I know it's not the best plan, but it's the best I got."

Stunned, she didn't know what to say. These two men were the only anchors she had in this world—without them, she would just fly away like a feather in the wind. The thought of staying with someone unknown made her feel nauseous. Who was this woman? How well did Khendric know her? How would she mistreat her? But the hardest blow was realising she burdened them, and they wanted to get rid of her.

"What do you think? As far as I remember, she's kind and takes good care of her employees."

"It. . . sounds like a good plan," she murmured.

Khendric had clearly put a lot of thought into this, and she didn't want to disappoint him.

"Great! I think you're going to make a fine nurse. When the day comes and some nasty beast claws my stomach open, you'll be the one to patch me back together." He chuckled, taking another sip.

"Like you'll need that," Topper said under his breath. It prompted a peculiar stare from Khendric. "It is a nine-day ride from here to Ashbourn."

She nodded, a tight knot forming in her stomach. *Only nine more days?*

"Err," a voice behind her sounded. "Master beast hunter?" Ara turned to see a ragged old man sitting alone at a table. He had a grey beard and hair, his clothes were filthy, and his posture crooked. "May I please trouble you for some time?"

"Yes, of course," Khendric said. The man sat opposite Khendric, and beside Topper.

"Thank you ever so much. I didn't know where else to turn and when I saw the giant heads mounted on your horses, I hoped you were beast hunters."

"Well, let's hope we can be of help," Khendric replied.

The old man looked to be on the verge of crying. "I believe there's something in my house," he said in a hushed tone. "But nobody believes me. I'm starving, and all my clothes are gone."

"Calm down, friend," Khendric said. "Start at the beginning. Why do you think there is something in your house?"

"Right, right, I'm sorry, it's just my mind has been a mess lately. Around three weeks ago, I noticed small changes in my house. First, pieces of food disappeared, a bit of grain here and some rice there. Then some meat vanished and a copper ring. I didn't notice it at first and just blamed my old mind, but eventually even I knew something was amiss." Topper scribbled some notes down as the old man talked. "One day I couldn't find my pocket watch, which I always have in either my pocket or on the bed stand. Then whole bags of rice disappeared—and all my clothes! Sometimes, at night, I thought I heard noises—barely audible footsteps in the living room—but when I entered no one was there. Now I'm afraid to enter my home at night. There's no food, and no clothes, and no one wants to help me. I have no family here that can aid either. I don't know what to do. Please, you have to help me." He began to sob holding his hands to his face.

Ara felt bad for thinking him dirty earlier.

"I see," Khendric said. "I will have to discuss this with my partner, mister. . .?"

"Robert."

"Well, Robert, you're in luck. We're still in the kingdom of Avania, which has a salary for official beast hunters. You'll need to sign a contract that I can take to Kalastra for payment. I didn't plan on going back there for quite some time, but luckily the contract won't expire for years."

"Do you mean it?" Robert asked, a tear rolling down his cheek. "You'll help me?"

"Well, as I said, I need to talk with my partner first. Can you wait by that table, and I'll call you over when we've reached a decision?" Khendric pointed to a table across the room.

"Yes," Robert replied, standing and wiping his tears on his sleeve.

"What do you think?" Topper asked, once the man was gone.

"Oh, I think lots of things," Khendric replied. "If what he says is true, there could be a beast or it could be regular human thieves. Even though it seems the items stolen were primarily food, it's still quite weird for a thief to steal from the same house repeatedly. However, we have another task at hand." He looked at Ara. "Getting you to Ashbourn. Therefore, it's up to you. For me it's all the same, we can stay and help the man, or we can carry on with our original plan. It's hard to say how long it will take. Could be up to a week, so it depends on you."

Her jaw dropped. She didn't know what to say.

My choice? He's letting me decide?

It felt unnatural. Her father had always made the decisions in her life. She realised Robert's life might be in her hands, and a sense of responsibility grasped her. The poor man looked so hungry and dirty. Staying and helping him benefited them both because she would have more time with Khendric and Topper, which made her feel better and safer. Also, she might learn what was haunting the house.

"We can stay," Ara said. "I want to help him."

"Alright, as long as you stay safe. You don't have to be in your room all the time, but don't stray too far from the inn," Khendric said.

It was as if a fire inside her extinguished. Khendric didn't want her to join on the actual mystery even though she had travelled with them for the past two weeks, setting up their camp, learning about different beasts and their dangers. Khendric had even given her his book about them. But it was clear, she was a burden. Even the woman in the beast hunter shop said it was rare to see a female beast hunter. She clearly had no place here with them.

"So what do you think it is?" Topper asked.

Khendric shrugged. "It could be many things."

Ara had a sour feeling in her stomach. "I. . ." She took a deep breath. "I want to help you." They both frowned, and she almost regretted speaking, but her lips kept moving. "I want to help you find the beast and help the old man."

"You do?" Khendric asked, surprised. "I thought you hated all this beast hunter stuff? You never really showed an interest in it, and I had to practically shove the book in your face."

"I really wanted to read it right away," she admitted. "I just didn't because I didn't want to seem too excited. And even though securing the camp is tedious, I loved learning about the beasts I've been protecting us against."

Khendric chuckled. "What do you say, Topper?"

"Ara," Topper said looking more serious that she had ever seen him. "We can't guarantee your safety."

"That's true," Khendric added. "Although we'll certainly do our best. Maybe you can observe the investigation, but if it becomes dangerous, you can leave, okay?"

Ara nodded excitedly.

Khendric grinned. "Who knows, maybe you'll like it and become a beast hunter."

"Is this how you become one?" Ara asked.

"Anyone can become a beast hunter, but it's tough and you obviously need to be very brave. Though, most people who do are often down on their luck or have no other option, so they decide to go fight monsters."

"Does everyone get a medallion?" she asked, making him frown questioningly. "I saw Topper's."

"Oh, did you? Few people get one. You need to be recognised by a capital, and to do that you need to have killed at least three medium-sized beasts, solved three cases—these two can go hand in hand—and pass an oral exam held by an official beast hunter."

"And do you think I could do that?" she asked, her eyes large and hopeful.

"If you stick around long enough," he said. "First you've got to find out if you like it." Khendric waved Robert over, and he hurriedly hobbled to their table.

"We'll help you," Khendric said.

"Really? You mean it?" Robert gasped before he hugged Khendric who laughed.

"Yes, of course. You can sleep in our room here at the inn tonight. But first, we need to get you bathed and fed."

Robert gazed at Khendric, dumbfounded. "That's so kind of you. You don't have to do all that."

"You seem like a decent man. And decent folk are hard to come by these days."

Robert's tears fell uncontrollably, and he put his forehead to the table, weeping.

"It's going to be alright," Khendric said kindly. "We'll start tomorrow, during the day. I need a good night's sleep, and it's probably safer then as well."

"No one has ever helped me. I truly had given up. I thought I was going to die, and no one would even notice." He leaned in and collapsed on Topper's shoulder. It was quite a sight.

Topper, presumably having no idea how to handle the situation, looked to Khendric and Ara for help. Khendric made slow stroking movements, mouthing, 'Comfort him'.

"There, there," Topper said, awkwardly petting Robert's head. "It'll be alright."

Something about this felt right. It was good to see what hope could do to this broken man's heart. Ara wished someone had given her hope after her sister Alena died, but instead there had only been misery. For the first time in a long time, she felt a sliver of hope for herself as well. The warmness grew inside her and, for once, she went to bed with a smile on her face.

CHAPTER 5

The Way of the Beast Hunter

Ara looked in the mirror as she brushed her hair and realised something had changed. There was a new glow in her cheeks. She felt better than ever, filled with renewed energy.

As Ara approached their room, she heard Khendric, Topper, and Robert's snoring through the thin wooden walls. She knocked on their door. No answer came, but that wasn't unexpected. She went in and shook them awake until, after a few seconds of protest, they roused from their slumber.

"I hope Robert's mystery turns out to be as exciting as you think." Khendric yawned. "But first, breakfast."

They all went down to the bar and sat at a table.

"So, there are no signs of any break-ins?" Khendric asked Robert as the old man sat down.

Robert shook his head. "No, not that I've seen. Suddenly stuff was just gone. Does that tell you anything?"

"It could be a group of shinies," Khendric said. "But you said clothes were taken too?"

Robert nodded.

"Not typical shiny behaviour," Topper mused.

"What are shinies?" Ara asked.

"Shinies are small creatures that steal all kinds of valuables. They're about the size of your hand, and rather cute, with their furry plump back and stump of a tail. But they're expert thieves, and often operate in groups. A true menace, especially if you're rich, but a simple trap should take care of them."

"But you don't think it's shinies?" she asked.

"No, because they only go for shiny items." Khendric turned to face Robert. "I mean no offence or ill will, but I have to ask. You mentioned you live alone—did you have a wife?"

Robert's face fell. "Yes, Morosel died about a year ago."

"I'm sorry for your loss. What killed her?" Khendric asked.

"Age. She was older than me by nine years."

"And there was no ill will between you?"

"Ill will?" Robert frowned.

"Fighting? Jealousy? Anything that could have driven a wedge between you?"

Robert leaned back, rubbing his chin. "Well, she did complain that I never cleaned enough, or that I never got rid of that damned tree-stump outside. My beard always annoyed her, which was why I kept it, as a tease. But she was rarely truly angry." His voice cracked on the last few words, and Ara noticed how his eyes filled with tears.

"I'm sorry to keep asking, but was there anyone else you've had any trouble with? A neighbour or maybe a jealous woman?"

"That's flattering, but I'm afraid I've never fared too well with the ladies. No, for me it was Morosel from an early age, and I have never had eyes for anyone else. I swear that on my life."

Once the plates were empty, Khendric ran his fingers through his black hair and put on his broad hat. Ara stood up in a flash, looking at him excitedly.

"I don't know what you find so exciting about this." Khendric chuckled. "But I'm loving this energy."

Topper put on his black sweater and a small, brown bag Ara hadn't seen before. Both he and Khendric had sheathed swords attached to their belts.

With Robert at the helm, Ara, Khendric, and Topper, walked through Cornstead, and she found she quite liked the village. The Rundown had been such a depressing place, while Cornstead teemed with life. People chatted on every corner and in every street, while children played with toys she'd never even dreamt of having as a child.

Khendric leaned closer as they walked. "Do you know why I asked Robert so many personal questions?"

Jolted from her admiration of Cornstead, she shook her head.

"I thought Robert might be dealing with a vengeful remnant," he explained. "A vengeful remnant is the ghost of someone he might have betrayed or killed in cold blood."

"But he's so sweet," she said.

"People often surprise you, and your assumptions could be your undoing," Khendric answered. "That's why it's better to ask those questions no matter how unlikely it feels. I've been wrong about people so many times."

Watching Robert a short distance ahead, she couldn't picture him lying, but perhaps that was exactly why she needed to learn this lesson.

When they neared Robert's street, the majority of the houses in the area appeared to be made with wood rather than the standard brick and mortar. It felt like stepping into another, less nice, village.

Most of the wooden houses were made to a higher standard than the brick ones, though occasionally a larger and more beautiful brick house emerged, with a larger yard and more windows. Those houses had a brick wall surrounding them designed to keep people out.

Robert's brick house did not have a wall and did not stand out in any way. He lived in the last row of smaller brick houses before reaching the forest beyond. These houses were packed in together and almost identical with minor differences you'd have to look really closely to spot. Robert's house had a small yard to one side with a tree-stump near the wooden fence.

"It's not big or grand," Robert said. "But it's mine. And I'm terrified of it."

"Let's hope we can change that," Khendric said.

"Why are these houses made from bricks and mortar rather than wood like all the others?" Ara asked.

"Partly tradition," Robert answered. "And partly because they're next to the forest, in case of forest fires."

Ara hadn't thought of that. Kalastra's forests were beyond the walls, so that was never an issue, though fires were still dangerous in her district.

The small party strolled across the yard, and Robert led them into the house which was empty. He walked them through all the rooms, explaining where many different items and family heirlooms should belong. The largest room had only a table, two chairs, and a wooden mixing bowl. In the bedroom, there were two roughly spun shirts, a pair of sandals, and a sheath for a dagger. From the pocket of his new trousers he found a small ruby.

"What you see in front of you, plus this ruby, is all I have left," Robert said. "It is the only valuable thing I have left in this world. It used to be set in a ring, but the thieves left the ruby behind and took the ring. If I only knew why."

Khendric thanked Robert for the tour of the house and sent him back to the inn.

"So, what do you think?" Ara asked, excitedly.

"I have many thoughts," Khendric answered, giving a sly smile. "But I'm interested in what *you* see." He gestured for her to look around the room. "Go on. I'll help you as best I can."

"Do you already know what it is?"

"I have no idea what it is," Khendric said, to Ara's relief. She wanted to solve this mystery—not by herself of course—or at least contribute in some way. "Now, look through the rooms and see what you find."

Her excitement quickly turned to frustration. She found nothing of significance in any of the rooms. No clear trace of fingerprints, hair, or anything else left by the culprit. She went outside and traced the outline of the property. Behind the house and outside the fence grew the forest.

This has to be the most concealed way to enter the house, she thought, examining the patch of grass between the house and the trees.

Khendric was leaning against the wall. "Anything?"

Ara grunted and kept looking, determined to find something—anything. The wooden fence seemed intact, with no footprints or other signs of disturbance.

"I was afraid it wouldn't be as much fun as you hoped." Khendric turned and went back inside the house. "Come along!"

Reluctantly, she followed. Khendric sat on a chair with Topper's bag in his hand.

"We're going to show you a secret." Khendric opened the bag and pulled out a syringe filled with orange liquid. "This is known as the paratis serum that we use often while investigating. It will enhance your senses. Come over here." He cleaned the needle while Ara waited reluctantly in the doorway. "It's only a little sting. I wanted you to try without the serum first, to make you appreciate it once the world is unlocked to you."

Khendric stuck the needle into his own shoulder and injected some of the liquid. "See? I'm fine." He replaced the needle with a fresh one and gestured for her to move closer.

"It's the exact same serum I'll give you, but it's a trade secret, for licenced beast hunters only. . . and you."

She prayed she could trust them, but her feet moved forward despite her uncertainty. Khendric touched the needle to her shoulder and she felt a slight sting.

He patted her on the back. "It will take effect very soon."

And it did. Her senses elevated to an incredible level. She smelled a pie being baked some houses away; the faeces left by an animal in the forest behind the house wafting through the open window; the dirt under Khendric's fingernails; the scent of the syringe; Topper's breath, which smelled like eggs; he was sweating—producing a saltier odour than Khendric.

"I think it's working," Topper said in a low voice.

The elevated sense of smell seemed dull in comparison with her new eyesight. She could see everything—absolutely *everything*. The impurities in their skin, the small strands of hair on Khendric's ear. Her eyes caught Topper's pores secreting drops of sweat, and each fibre of fabric making up his sweater.

"What is this?" she said with a low voice, gazing at her hands. The veins under her skin practically glowed, revealing all the different patterns in her palms. Her blood rushed through her veins, contrasting with Khendric and Topper's heartbeats. The floorboards moved slightly in response to their movement. Her clothes scraped uncomfortably against her skin.

"It's. . ." her voice rang through her head like a mighty church bell. She lowered her voice. "It's *amazing*."

"We wanted you to search for clues without it first," Topper said. "Now it should be much easier, and you'll appreciate the serum a lot more."

Ara searched the room and her jaw dropped. She could see every crack in the wooden floor and ceiling and all the different colours outside the window. The world was full of fantastic, vibrant colours that she had never noticed before. The grass was countless different shades of green. She caught her breath. Never had she dreamt of seeing the world so clearly.

"This is what you hid in the pouch," Ara realised, turning back to Khendric. "When you disappeared into the woods." He nodded. "Is this what gave you the fiery pupils?"

"Just like you have now."

"I do?" She wished she could see herself, but there was no mirror here.

"Look into my eyes," Khendric said, and as she did, she saw her own glowing, orange pupils reflected. The fire inside her eyes danced beautifully. Learning beast hunter secrets was so much fun, she couldn't help smiling.

"What if I don't find anything?" she asked.

"Then I'll have a look after," Khendric said. "What are you waiting for? Get snooping."

She went over to the window closest to the forest and inspected it. Nothing escaped her elevated vision. She waved them over.

"The frame has clear patches of dust and small splinters. Also, I am pretty sure the wood itself is pressed down slightly here as if someone or something stood on the frame."

Topper wrote down everything she said on a piece of parchment.

"Nice one, Ara," Khendric said.

She continued to look through the room and close to a corner, she spotted a strand of hair. She carefully picked it up. "I found this." Khendric leaned in and saw it too. "It's black."

"Could be Topper's," Khendric said.

"No, Topper's hair is a completely different shade of black. It doesn't belong to him."

"Impressive," Khendric said.

Topper brought forth a small vial and let Ara place the hair inside.

"Do you know what kind of beast or beasts we're dealing with?" she asked.

"I have some ideas to what it isn't, at least," Khendric said. "But let's see if there are any more clues before the effect of the serum wears off."

"How long is it going to last?"

"You should have around another twenty minutes."

"Oh," Ara said. She scouted the room again. "The intruder must have come in through the window, but our walking in the grass has wiped away any clues."

She went to the door and opened it. The strong sunlight shocked her, and she had to shield her eyes. Behind the house the sunlight was weaker as she examined the potential crime scene. She lifted her gaze and looked at the overhanging trees. The branches leading to the house were bent slightly and the number of pine needles didn't look as thick there compared to the rest of the tree.

"I think whatever it was used the branches to get to the window."

"Clever," Khendric answered. "Many people forget to look up—I'm impressed you did."

She smiled and felt the warmness yet again in her chest. "I want to go back inside."

"Then that's what we'll do."

"You should really remove those grey hairs from your ear," she said as she passed. "They're disgusting."

He grabbed his ear, and Ara laughed out loud.

"That's what I hate about that damn serum," Khendric muttered.

Inside she found the remaining items and looked at them with new eyes. The mixing bowl seemed untouched, so did the sandals and the two shirts. She inspected the dagger sheath.

"Nothing," she said, putting it down, but she noticed something wasn't quite right. In the darkness of the sheath's cavity was something reflecting a tiny fraction of light. She stuck her fingers in and found yet another strand of hair—white as snow.

"Nice," Topper said, producing another vial.

"This could be Robert's hair," Ara said. "But without him, I can't differentiate this strand from his hair."

"True," Topper answered. "It's worth looking into."

"So, two strands of hair with completely different colours," Khendric noted. "That means there is potentially more than one perpetrator, if the white hair doesn't belong to Robert. This is good enough for now, Ara," Khendric reassured her. "We've got some things to work on."

Though she didn't want to stop, he was right. She was beginning to feel exhausted as the effects of the paratis serum began to fade. They headed for the door as a gust of wind rolled over her, a peculiar smell entering her nostrils.

"Wait! I smell something."

The two looked at her expectantly.

She sniffed the air, and the scent grew stronger when she neared the curtains. "There's something here." A vague dark pattern stained the fabric.

Khendric leaned close. "What is that?"

"It looks like... soot," Ara said. "But it has a very distinct and weird smell."

Khendric hit the curtain and particles of soot were thrust into the air.

"Maybe it's some kind of spore?" Topper suggested.

"Probably," Khendric said.

"Spore?" Ara asked.

"A kind of dust emitted by flowers, trees, and even some beasts," Topper explained.

"Like a mildwever. The little bastards find crops and go to sleep in them, then in their slumber, they emit spores that kill the crop. They're a great pain for farmers but this doesn't look like mildwever spores. I think theirs is a yellow-brown colour," Khendric said.

These spores were not even close to yellow-brown, but dark—almost black. Ara leaned in to get a better hold of the scent. It was overwhelming, and she coughed as it scratched the back of her throat.

"Oh," Khendric said. "That was probably not too clever."

"Huh?" she said between coughs.

"Well spores can affect humans, and I don't know what kind of spores these are. Do you feel okay?"

"Yes, besides the itchy throat."

"That might be all," Khendric said. "We'll have to keep an eye on you and tell us about anything you find unusual, alright?"

She nodded and drank the water Topper handed to her.

"Let's head back, then. We should discuss what we have found—maybe you'll learn a thing or two."

Ara nodded. Her head was starting to feel fuzzy, and she wanted to lay down. Her performance had seemed perfect, up until smelling the spores.

They closed and locked the door with the key Robert had given them and left.

CHAPTER 6
The Warning

"Ara, please wake up." The voice was barely audible.

"Did she just move?" Another voice. She recognised this one too.

Who are these people? Where are my parents?

Ara slowly opened her heavy eyelids and saw two blurry shapes in an unfamiliar room.

"Thank the stonepudders," a man with dark skin and short hair said. That was about the only thing she could make out about him. He removed a patch of cloth from her forehead. "Ara, are you okay?"

They know my name. Where are my parents?

Her vision slowly came into focus. Two men were watching her, concerned "M—my parents?" she said, her voice raspy.

"Do you remember us, Ara?" the lanky man asked. "It's me, Topper."

"I'm Khendric." He turned away from her and in a gentle voice said, "Your parents were killed by a rura."

It all flooded back: the attack, her parents' mangled bodies, her saviours, arriving in Cornstead, Robert, and finally Robert's house. Tears welled behind her eyes and cascaded down her cheeks.

"What h—happened to me?"

"We don't know," Khendric said. "You smelled the spores and, on the way back to the inn, you... I don't know how to explain it but it's like you stopped functioning."

Stopped functioning?

They helped her sit upright so she was leaning against the headboard. She slowly flexed her hands.

"What's the last thing you remember?" Topper asked.

"Umm, we were walking back to the inn and... nothing."

"We think the spores affected you," Khendric said. "On our way home, you stopped moving forward, and stood still like you were frozen. You didn't respond to anything we said or did, and I had to carry you to your bed."

"What? You had to carry me? I don't remember any of that." Her breathing quickened and her heart beat harder. What if she'd been with someone else? What if someone wanted to harm her?

"How do you feel?" Topper asked.

"Tired and worried," she answered. "And I have a headache. How long have I been out?"

"A couple of hours," Khendric said. "Evening is approaching."

She curled her toes a couple of times and proceeded to stand up. Besides being a little wobbly at first, she was okay. "Can I have some water?"

Topper handed her a flask, and she drank from it, feeling instantly refreshed.

"What about the case?" Ara asked

"What about it?" Khendric frowned.

"What do we do now?"

He scoffed. "Are you serious? I don't think you're in any shape to do much."

"I'll be fine. Trust me, I've been in much worse states than this, and still went to the market for my parents."

"I still think we're done for the day," Topper said, glancing at Khendric.

"Do you have any other suspects for Robert's house?"

Khendric and Topper shared a look.

"Well," Khendric began. "I was thinking it could be witchtrolls."

"I've never heard of them," Ara said.

"Witchtrolls are small, female, humanoid creatures. They're intelligent and resourceful, even knitting clothes for themselves and doing magic. We think it could be witchtrolls because they steal items from a person to curse them."

"Curse them?" Ara wondered.

"That's right. They curse people with bad luck or influence their minds to do sinister things. The worst part is that they seem to do it purely for entertainment."

"But would they steal food?"

"Often," Topper said, taking off his sweater which he hung over the end of her bed.

"So, you think it is them?" she asked.

"Witchtrolls often work in groups, but would never steal this much, and Robert doesn't seem to be struck with any bad luck lately, except for being robbed, of course." Khendric sighed. "Which makes me think it's unlikely. Plus they don't produce spores as far as we know."

Ara walked slowly to the window. She pulled it up, relieved that the strength had returned to her arms. A comfortable breeze washed over her. She closed her eyes, enjoying the fresh air on her skin when a horrible scream rang through the room from outside.

Her eyes snapped open and she peered outside but it was so dark that she couldn't see anything. "What was that?"

"It sounded like a woman," Khendric said, joining her at the window.

"Should we check it out?" she asked.

"Are you sure you're okay?"

"Yes," she said, turning to get her jacket. "Maybe it's connected to the case."

"That's highly unlikely," Khendric said, but he still put on his hat and coat.

"We don't need to check it out, do we?" Topper said.

"I'm up for it if Ara is," Khendric said. "I like mysteries."

"I do too," Topper said. "But I also like sleep, and I'm exhausted, and so are you. We have enough on our plate."

"What if it is connected?" Ara said. "It's just a headache. I want to check it out."

"I'm going to get some sleep." Topper pouted at them and folded his arms.

"Let's go," Khendric said with a grin.

When Ara and Khendric left the inn, the streets were empty except for a few people scurrying towards the frantic voices in the distance. Another sharp scream cut through the air. Ara and Khendric glanced at each other and, without a word, they ran towards the sound. A crowd had already gathered so Khendric fished out his medallion and flashed it at everyone to allow Ara and him through. Ara caught fragments of conversation from the people who were talking in hushed voices.

"Another one?"

"This happened again?"

They reached the crime scene to find a man laying still on the ground, bleeding from his chest. Next to him were two others who both appeared to be dead. One wore a beautiful purple dress. It was hard to tell if it was a woman or a man because the head was split open, a slurry of hair, blood, and brains mingling with the mud. People were being sick, and Ara had to look away. Beside the body in the dress, was a dead man whose torso and head were covered in bloody lesions. More and more people vomited onto the muddy ground, and the overpowering smell forced Ara to concentrate hard on not following suit.

Ara's eyes wandered to a man holding a bloody sword in his hand. He wore a tight black uniform.

"Who's that?" she asked.

"I think he's a constable," Khendric answered. "Here's what I think happened: The constable killed the first man, the aggressor, who most likely killed the woman in the dress. Her husband probably tried to either attack or defend himself against said aggressor but was murdered before the constable could help.

More constables arrived at the scene, trying to get the bystanders to move along. Two men carried the aggressor away on a stretcher.

"This is peculiar," Khendric said, standing his ground.

"I heard some talk, and I don't think it's the first time this has happened." Ara glanced around them.

"Do you want to investigate? I don't think this is linked, but—"

"I do," Ara said quickly.

"Okay, come on."

They trailed the constables back past the inn, through the marketplace, and to what must have been the morgue before stopping in a small alleyway sprouting from the main road. Leaning against the wall, with Khendric by her side, Ara eyed the morgue. She felt like a spy. Footsteps approached them from behind, and they turned around in a flash. Khendric pointed his pistol at a small individual in the shadows.

"Khendric?"

Ara recognised the voice, but from where?

"That's you, right?" Khendric remained silent, and so did Ara. "And Ara, I met you earlier."

"You're the woman from the beast hunter store," Ara said.

"Yes, and I must talk to you Master Beast Hunter. I am Horana Takenzi." She stepped out from the shadows, lit by a nearby lantern.

"Pleasure to meet you, Horana," he said.

"I come bearing grim news. Something vile is happening to the village. I can only speak of what I've seen myself, but people are changing. Good people have been acting strangely."

"Strangely?" he asked.

"Like the scene you just witnessed. The man who killed that couple was a blacksmith. He was renowned for his tools and crafting skills, and his kindness. My people and I have known him for many years, and he was always stable and reliable. W—what he did today. . ." her voice broke, ". . . is not something he would have done in his right mind. There has been a rise in violence lately, most of it caused by individuals like Adriac the blacksmith."

"And you think these crimes are linked?" Khendric asked.

Ara listened intently. *Another mystery,* she thought. *Maybe now I can get to spend more time with them.*

"Most definitely," Horana said. "In the last month, there have been twelve assaults like these, many by good men who've suddenly become monsters."

"That's a lot in one month. Any idea what might be causing it?"

"It's been gnawing on my mind and I have studied various books but found nothing. I don't know of any beast that can cause so many people to become maniacal and yet remain so well hidden."

"That's what I was thinking too," Khendric agreed. "Manipulation on a scale like this should leave traces."

"Exactly! Yet I have found nothing. But I have not done much investigative work either."

"I see," Khendric said. "Any particular pattern to these attacks?"

"I haven't been able to pinpoint anything. It seems random. The first was outside the city, a lumberjack. Two in the marketplace, and others in different districts."

"Hmm and what about the location of the subject's houses? Any patterns?"

"I've not checked into that."

"Can you?" Khendric asked and Horana nodded. "Meanwhile, we'll see what we can find in the morgue. Have only men been affected?"

"No, two women also—one my age, and the other quite young, but I believe more than two women *may* have been affected. Women are changed differently. There have been reports of them becoming completely docile."

"Docile?" Khendric asked, shooting a glance at Ara.

She made the connection too, meeting his eyes.

"Yes, submissive," Horana continued. "I've not seen it for myself, only heard the rumours. Apparently, they won't eat, or drink, or move, they just stand about, their mind seemingly blank. Unfortunately, I don't know more than that."

Exactly what happened to me, Ara thought.

"Did the women recover?" she asked.

"Yes, but it took some days."

Days? That's peculiar.

"Thank you," Khendric said. "If what you say is true, you have been very helpful."

"Please look into this," Horana pleaded.

"We will. Do what I asked, and I will do what I can also."

"Thank you, Master Beast Hunter," she said. "Come to my shop when you have time." She turned around and disappeared into the darkness of the alley.

Khendric tucked the pistol back into his belt and they strolled along the street towards the morgue. When they arrived, Khendric simply walked through the door, and Ara followed, trying not to show her nervousness. The room was large, with countless coffins stacked against the walls. Two constables wearing the same tight dark uniforms Ara had seen earlier, sat on barstools behind a small counter, blocking a door.

"Hey!" one bellowed. "You can't be here!" He was a plump man, his beard covering only his neck. Beside him, a thin man with a bony face and wispy dark hair was reading a book.

They both had a constable's medallion hanging from their constable's shirts which Ara guessed to be official proof of their authority. While Khendric's was round, theirs were square with an intricate pattern. The plump man rose from his chair and took a step towards Khendric.

"Good evening, constables," Khendric said, tipping his hat as he continued towards them.

"Stop!" the plump man said. Khendric leaned on the counter, while Ara waited by his side. "Who are you?"

"I'm a mortician," Khendric said easily. "And this is my assistant."

"You—you are?"

"No they aren't," the skinny officer said, rolling his eyes. "You buffoon."

"I thought it worth a try," Khendric said, winking at the plump man, who glanced back and forth between the two. "I'm a beast hunter and a good one at that. She is my apprentice."

"Oh. Well, are you allowed to be here then?" the plump man asked.

"In the morgue?" Khendric asked, frowning.

"They're allowed to be here," the bony one said. "But they're not allowed to pass. Being a beast hunter doesn't grant them that authority."

"What's your name?" Khendric asked the plump man.

"Morta."

"Well, Morta, I think we can shed some light on this murder. Even better, we'll give you guys all the credit, and you can brag about it to your supervisor."

"What do you mean 'shed some light'?" the skinny man said. "It was murder, simple as that." He stared down at the book he was reading.

"As simple as that?" Khendric asked. "A murder? You believe the calm and renowned blacksmith suddenly went on a rampage and killed two people?"

The skinny man lifted his gaze slightly, glaring at Khendric before looking back at his book. "Yeah, could happen."

"Y—you don't think this crime is rather peculiar?" Ara said, feeling all eyes in the room suddenly upon her.

"You know what?" the constable said, putting the book down. "Life can become complicated if you overthink stuff like this or ask too many questions."

"But you're a constable. This is your job!" Khendric said.

"No. My job is to sit here and make sure you don't enter to do all your beast hunter-stuff."

"You mean the stuff that might help you solve this crime?"

"There's nothing to solve! Now turn around and leave!"

"Martyn," Morta said. "Please stop."

"Nothing to solve?" Khendric asked. "You mean to tell me that the rise in murders this past month is coincidental?" Martyn frowned in response. "You don't find it weird that there have been twelve murders, many in the same style as this one when, before that, I bet you barely saw a single murder? Don't you want to know who's behind it?"

Morta nodded. "Mr Kontho, our superior, did say he wanted to discover what was linking these murders."

"Morta!" Martyn snapped.

"What? I heard it, I swear. Before he rode off today."

"Well then," Khendric continued, "I can give you something to tell Mr. Kontho that could potentially solve the case. That could mean a handsome reward for two handsome officers."

"Alright! You have ten minutes. Any longer, I'll arrest you for interfering with the law."

Khendric walked past them with a chuckle, and Ara followed, trying not to look apologetic. They went down a staircase and found a mortician working on the dead blacksmith. Khendric fished out his medallion as the man looked up.

"Ah, I prayed a beast hunter would arrive in Cornstead soon." The mortician was an elderly man, with a shiny bald head. He had a slim, robust face and wore spectacles and a brown leather apron.

"Glad someone is happy to see us. I'm Khendric, and this is Ara, my apprentice."

"Nice to meet you, I'm Nadam." He took off his spectacles and rubbed his hands together before offering his right hand to her.

She shook it. "Nice to meet you. Have you found anything?"

Nadam smiled. "You're eager. That's good." He sighed and placed both hands on the table. "No. I have opened each of these bodies up, and I've had no luck figuring it out. I don't know how up to speed you are?"

"We have gathered enough information."

"Great. Because of their maniacal behaviour, all twelve perpetrators were killed, and none of them had any obvious signs pointing to their drastically increased aggression. I've inspected their intestines and found nothing out of the ordinary. I opened their skulls, examined their brains, but all was well." He wiped his forehead and sighed heavily. "So now I'm stuck here with yet another corpse and no explanation to give to Mr. Kontho."

Khendric gazed over the opened blacksmith studying his insides. "Have you opened his stomach? Perhaps he ate something?"

"Yes. I thought of that. None of the subjects had anything suspicious, or even anything in common with regards to the contents of their stomachs."

Despite the smell, Ara felt more comfortable here than upstairs, as Nadam didn't want to stop them from investigating, but instead welcomed their help. She hoped the constables wouldn't cause them more trouble.

Khendric crossed his arms and frowned. "And their hearts were fine?"

"That's the only thing they all have in common. There's a slight enlargement of the heart muscle in every one of them, but it's difficult to conclude anything. The heart seems a bit bruised and battered, but this aligns with the great effort required to carry out a brutal murder."

"But no black spots?" Khendric asked.

"No, no discolouration. So any help you can give is appreciated."

"We *might* be able to do something, but I would prefer if we could be alone."

"Oh," Nadam said. "Yes, of course. Just be careful with the bodies."

"You have my word." Khendric smiled at the man.

After Nadam left, Khendric put his hat on the table and turned to Ara. "How are you doing?"

"I'm okay. I'm so glad we went to investigate."

Khendric smiled. "Yeah, that was the right call." He glanced around to make sure they were alone. "I told Nadam to leave because I was thinking we could use paratis serum to help investigate."

"Smart," she said. "Could you inject me?"

He injected a small dose into her shoulder before doing the same to himself. Ara's senses instantly heightened. There was a strong smell of death, and Ara had to focus her attention on not throwing up.

They both examined Adriac. Under his nails was only what appeared—and smelled—like human skin.

"The intestines also appear normal," Khendric whispered.

The sight was staggering and threatened to overwhelm her, but she fought to stay focused on the mystery and not the disgusting details she saw in the blacksmith's guts. Khendric checked Adriac's eyes by rolling them around in their sockets and gave her a thumbs-up to indicate nothing was wrong.

She inhaled and. . . smelled *something*, a weird smell that shouldn't exist in a corpse, yet was familiar to her. "The spores. I smell them."

As she passed the face, the scent surfaced again, coming from Adriac's nose. She found a piece of cloth, wrapped it around a small stick, and slowly inserted it into Adriac's left nostril. It was lightly stained with dark soot when Ara removed it.

"These are the same spores from Robert's house."

"I have to admit, that is quite peculiar," Khendric said.

"Do you think these spores are dangerous?" she asked.

Khendric shook his head. "No. This is from a secondary source, and there's so little of it."

Footsteps approached the door, and a second later, Nadam entered the room. Khendric handed Ara two small pieces of rubber from his coat pocket. "For your ears," he whispered, "and hide your eyes." Khendric pulled his hat down, making sure the rim hid his flaming eyes.

Hide my eyes? How do I hide my eyes?

"Is it safe for me now?" Nadam asked. His words rang loudly in Ara's ears, like glass shattering inside her head. She squeezed the pieces of rubber into her ears.

"It is," Khendric said.

"What have you for me, Master Beast Hunter and apprentice?" Nadam asked, rubbing his hands together and walking toward them.

Ara pointedly looked in the other direction. She must've appeared foolish, but what else could she do?

"We found this in his nose," Khendric said.

Ara dared to look as Nadam fixated on the piece of cloth. The mortician held it up to a nearby lantern and Ara had to look away so as not to get blinded. "Very peculiar. That should not be there."

"Do you have any other subjects here?" Khendric asked. "We can check them as well."

"I'm afraid the authorities don't let me keep them very long. They're a superstitious lot, but who can blame them? Usually, after two or three days, they put them in coffins. They're so afraid the corpses might spread disease. I'm even scared they're going to put me in one some days!"

"I see," Khendric murmured. "If by chance, something like this happens again. . ."

"I will check," Nadam said.

"Great. As long as we can get past constable Martyn, I will return as fast as I can."

"He's had an unfortunate history with beast hunters and his parents—a long story. I will talk to Mr. Kontho about letting you pass."

"Thank you," Khendric answered, turning to leave.

The effects of the paratis serum faded, the dullness of the real world emerging once again, so Ara removed the rubber pieces from her ears, and she no longer had to fear showing her eyes. But the strong smell abated too.

Martyn and Morta, were still stationed in the hallway when Ara and Khendric walked past them towards the door.

"So? What did you find?" Martyn asked.

"Oh, nothing." Khendric replied with a smile. He didn't slow down and Ara followed in his wake.

"But you said—" Martyn tried to protest, but they were already out the door, walking through the empty streets towards the inn.

Ara couldn't help but smile. Not answering the constables gave her a feeling of power, something her life had lacked in many years.

CHAPTER 7
So Many Possibilities

Ara awoke as sunlight shone brightly on her eyelids. Her head still hurt, but not nearly as much as yesterday. She sat up in her bed and rubbed her eyes, before getting dressed.

She left her room and knocked on the door of the room shared by Khendric, Topper, and Robert. Topper let her in, and she frowned at the mess. She could almost see picture father's disgust at such a sight. Topper's bed was a mess, and his nightstand full of random stuff: pencils, a knife, empty vials, two small books, and several crumpled papers. Khendric slept soundly in his bed, face buried in his pillow, and sheets halfway on the floor. Robert slept on a small couch.

Ara couldn't help but notice Khendric's perfect skin—no marks, scars, or impurities.

I'd never take him for a beast hunter, she thought.

He looked like he'd never been in a fight. One would think a man like him would have lived through a few scarring ordeals.

"How are you feeling?" Topper asked her.

"A minor headache, but I feel great."

"Are you hungry?"

She discovered her appetite was greater than she first thought. "I am."

They left the room with Robert and Khendric snoring heavily inside and found a table downstairs in the bar.

* * *

Khendric joined them just as she was finishing her meal in his usual hat and coat. He went to speak to the innkeeper before seating himself at their table.

"Good morning," Ara said. "I was about to tell Topper of our discoveries last night."

"Khendric already told me," Topper said.

"Okay, so what do we do now?" she wondered.

The innkeeper passed them carrying several plates of food. He handed one to Khendric as he flew by.

"We eat, and talk," Khendric answered. "Perhaps it's a vengeful remnant."

"The thing you talked about yesterday with Robert?" she asked. Khendric nodded.

"But Robert said he and his wife had a great relationship and he had no enemies."

"First rule you need to learn is it's not wise to take Robert's word as fact when it comes to vengeful remnants. Everything he said could be true, but it could also be a lie."

"Why would anyone lie to a beast hunter? You're there to help."

"I don't know," Khendric said. "Many people value their honour more than their life. A man without honour is no man's friend."

"I see," Ara said.

"Wait," Topper chimed in. "So, you get to quote a saying, but I don't?"

"Mine are actually good, so yeah."

She chuckled. "So, do you think Robert was lying?"

"Personally, no, but you never know. Vengeful remnants are created from a murder so unjust that the victim's feeling of betrayal is beyond our comprehension. Then it haunts its murderer, starting with simple things: nightmares, missing or broken items. It quickly gets worse. Mirrors break, knives go flying, until the remnant grows strong enough through time to attack. These attacks can severely injure the person, or even kill them."

"How do you stop it?" Ara asked, leaning forward.

"Usually, burning the bones of the dead works," Khendric said. "But it's no guarantee. If it doesn't work, you need to destroy an item important to the deceased and hope you find the right one in time."

"I see," Ara said. A vengeful remnant didn't seem probable. Robert hadn't mentioned any bad dreams or sightings of his dead wife. "I don't think it's a vengeful remnant either. It would be weird for a ghost to steal this many items. A valuable heirloom or a ring would make sense, but not all the plates, food, clothes, and so on, and especially without seeming to escalate to more aggressive actions."

"Those are my thoughts as well."

"Yesterday, when you were out," Topper said, "I went to ask Robert's neighbours about his wife. Everyone I met said they had a great relationship so I don't think it's a vengeful remnant either."

"What else can it be?" Ara asked looking from Khendric to Topper.

Khendric leaned back on his chair. "I have some theories. Have you read about gremliks?" Ara shook her head. Khendric turned to Topper. "Do you want to fill her in?"

"Gremliks are humanoid, dark-green creatures with long nails on both hands and feet. They have two long ears and two smaller ones next to each other. Their teeth are usually in poor condition and as yellow as their eyes," Topper said.

"How big are they?" she asked.

"About half your height. Gremliks wear whatever they find, which is often quite humorous."

"Wait!" she said. "I think I've seen gremliks in Kalastra, but I didn't know what they were."

"You probably did," Topper said. "What they do is present themselves to a human begging for food, hoping to appeal to our sympathetic side. But if they're given too much food, they get greedy and come back for more. Then if you were to stop, they become aggressive and steal food or items."

Doesn't seem impossible, Ara thought. *Robert would have mentioned seeing a gremlik though, or maybe he didn't notice the beast revealing itself to him? I can picture a gremlik sneaking in through the window, using the branches, but what about the two different hair colours? Maybe gremliks have different shades of hair?*

The endless questions gnawed away at her. She thought gremliks were the kind of creatures to have warts and hair growing from weird places, considering their yellow eyes and bulky body.

"What are you thinking?" Khendric asked.

"Robert didn't mention seeing one. But maybe he overlooked the gremlik presenting itself to him. For all we know he could have bad eyesight."

"Yeah, that's a good point. I didn't think of that. We'll ask him."

Had she just thought of something Khendric hadn't? She couldn't stop her lips from curling into a quick smile. "Can a gremlik steal to provoke or get more food? And is it weird for a Gremlik to steal all of his belongings?"

Khendric nodded. "Kind of, yeah."

"So maybe there is more than one gremlik involved? You can multiply the amount usually stolen by however many gremliks there are. That could maybe explain the different shades of hair I found too—if gremliks have hair of course."

Khendric shot Topper a look. "I have to say I am impressed. It's not impossible. Though the only time I've heard of gremliks assembling is to specifically attack, but who knows? Maybe they've developed a scheme together. There is something weird and unlikely about this whole situation."

"It doesn't explain the ruby though," Topper added.

"No, a gremlik wouldn't leave a ruby but take the rest of the ring," Khendric said. "I don't have an explanation for that. Do either of you?"

Ara and Topper shook their head.

"The best ideas come to mind when reflecting events with others," Topper said.

"That isn't some profound saying, you stonepudder. That's just common sense."

"Umm. . . yeah, well. . ."

Khendric barked out a laugh.

"I'm *not* going to write that one down," Topper said, but he was grinning.

"It still doesn't explain the spores," Khendric said. "I have one last suggestion, but it seems even more unlikely. Perhaps it could be a spiderling?"

Topper leaned closer. "They're basically a large spider that live in homes until they outgrow them. That's when they kill and eat the unsuspecting residents and leave for the woods."

"That's terrible," Ara said, alarmed. "Could it be a spiderling then?"

"When they are young, they're quite mischievous, often stealing food and items for fun." Topper shrugged.

"They sound creepy," Ara said.

"And they are," Khendric agreed. "Nasty, crawling things, too quick for their own good. I once ended up burning down a family home just to kill one. The amount of food stolen means it would be large enough to kill Robert but I'm sure a spiderling would never leave—"

"Spores," Ara interjected.

"Exactly!"

With wide eyes, realisation dawned upon her. "There isn't one beast involved in this crime, but *two*!"

Khendric snapped his fingers and tapped his temple. "You're clever, Ara." He pulled a map from his coat pocket. "After we came back last night, I marked on this map where all the recent murderers lived. We'll visit one of these houses and see what we find, and hopefully, learn something new."

"But there's one thing I don't understand," Ara said. "If the spores were at Robert's house, why didn't he go all crazy like Adriac?"

Khendric slowly let out a breath. "I'm not sure. Maybe we'll find out."

Ara was already standing, more eager than ever to continue the investigation.

CHAPTER 8
Shedding New Light

The street outside the inn buzzed with life—merchants shouting prices, children playing, and hardworking people taking a quick break in the sun. The words 'murders', 'crazy', and 'Adriac', often broke through the general chatter. Though the mood seemed pleasant at first glance, worry resided in people's eyes.

Ara had Khendric's map in hand, but he grabbed it off her.

"The map was just to show you the pattern in which the murderer's houses were placed," Khendric said, putting a hand on her shoulder, before she went to protest. "I know the way." He rolled up the map and slid it back into one of his many pockets. "Follow me and you'll get to investigate real soon, I promise."

After walking through many streets, they arrived at a house about the same size as Robert's, in a densely populated area. It had no fence, and the roof connected with the two adjoining houses. The wooden walls desperately needed to be repaired, and the door had so many cracks it barely offered privacy. A dilapidated shed missing its door held several tools: hammers, pinches, knives, gloves, and more. Between the shed and house stood a rusty anvil.

"This is Adriac's house?" Ara asked.

Khendric nodded. "It is."

Topper peeked through both windows, before trying the door. To their surprise it creaked open and Topper went in first. Ara wanted to follow, but Khendric placed a hand on her shoulder.

"Let him scope it out first."

After a few minutes, Topper opened the door again. "It's clear."

Ara walked in to find it was the complete opposite of Robert's house. Papers, books, shoes, all sorts of half-rotten food, and clothes, were scattered on the floor. There was a blotch of spilt ink on the dining room table. Ara stepped carefully so as not to trip over all the rubble littering the ground.

Khendric examined the window frames but said nothing as he left the room.

"Nothing appears to have been stolen," Topper said. "No," she agreed, picking up some silver chips. "And probably no shinies, gremliks, or spiderlings either."

Khendric came back and leaned close to them. "I haven't found any of the clues we found in Robert's house."

They searched further but didn't find anything.

"Inject yourself with paratis serum," Khendric said after some time, giving Ara a syringe.

She steeled her nerves, closed her eyes, and pushed the needle into her shoulder. The sting wasn't bad. She waited a few seconds for the serum to take effect. Like before, all her senses elevated to incredible levels and Ara saw myriad shades of colour. At first, she relished the effects—then remembered she had a job to do.

Khendric was searching the living room and Topper the hallway, so Ara went to the kitchen. All the different foods blitzed her sense of smell. She smelled them individually and could separate them one by one, but somewhere in between all those aromas, she found a whiff of what she was searching for.

If the spores are here, don't inhale them, she reminded herself.

She used her enhanced eyesight instead, studying the different food items first, but they all seemed fine. She picked up a spoon and examined it closely, spotting some vague dark spots on the spoon's surface. She found the same spots on knives and forks, too. To be sure, she held a piece of cloth in front of her nostrils and smelled the spoon. The odour was strong and definitely the same spores found at Robert's house.

"Guys!" she yelled, almost deafening herself, her words ringing through her head like large bells. Khendric and Topper rushed in, also clutching their ears. "I found the spores." She pointed at the cutlery.

"Good job, Ara," Khendric said. "This confirms our earlier suspicions. There are two different beasts at work."

They searched another house, this one belonging to Peris Katharos, a tavern owner, who had gone on a killing spree suddenly and without any provocation. The situation was precisely the same: nothing stolen, but Topper found traces of spores on some mugs.

"We should go back to Robert's house," Ara suggested when they were done. "Maybe a fresh look would do us some good ignoring the spores."

Khendric looked to Topper.

"Okay, maybe ignoring the spores will shed some new light on the case. Let's go," Topper said.

On the way to Robert's house something occurred to Ara. These last few days she hadn't been afraid to ask questions, speak her ideas, ask for food, or just generally talk, and she had never felt freer. She couldn't pinpoint precisely why her behaviour had changed so much, but she *liked* it. Khendric and Topper seemed to respond well to it, and she felt much closer to them. Plus, they hadn't mentioned nursing again and she was careful not to bring it up. It was a good feeling, like she had reclaimed pieces of herself she feared would be lost forever.

They reached the brick house and headed inside with Robert's key.

"I brought the clues," Topper said removing them from a satchel. He put them on Robert's table: sandals, the ruby, dagger sheath, two vials containing the strands of hair, and two shirts.

Nothing new seemed to have been stolen, not that there was much left to steal. There were coat hangers, a table, two chairs, and a mixing bowl. Ara sat on a chair and looked at the clues. Topper sat beside her, and Khendric walked around the rooms, examining the other items.

She first examined the sandals, but they gave her nothing. She picked up the ruby, this clue bugging her the most.

Who would leave a ruby, but take the ring? There were tiny scratch marks on the ruby, from where the ring had held it in place. *Who would go to such efforts to remove such a fine gem?*

It seemed an unsolvable riddle for the time being, so she put it back on the table.

The two roughly spun shirts didn't offer any new information either. The dagger sheath was next, and she tried to go through the clues all together.

Someone took the dagger, but didn't need the sheath, maybe because they already had one? Then they—or it—removed the ruby from a ring, leaving behind the ruby. They took the shoes, but not the sandals. So, we're dealing with something armed with a dagger, wearing a ruby-less ring, dressed in Robert's working boots. . .

She pictured the most odd-looking man before sighing and walking to the rear of Robert's house, facing the forest. Leaning on the fence with his stone house behind her, she spotted bits of what looked like the wooden fence encircling the whole village.

She found it strange that parts of the great forest outside Cornstead had been walled off.

There must be good reason for it, she decided.

The forest was rugged with varied vegetation and giant trees that obscured the view. Ara thought she could spot a slight hill within the forest but wasn't sure. The wooden bar she leaned on collapsed, and she lurched forward, ending up hanging hunched over the second bar in the fence. She straightened and noticed the bar hadn't snapped—instead, it had loosened from the poles.

That's a weak fence, she thought and studied the rods which held the bars in place.

On the ground she spotted two wooden nails. They were crude and rotten. She examined the rest of the fence and found nothing but wooden nails in poor condition, and three bars held together by only a piece of cloth tied around them.

She jumped over the fence and went to inspect the neighbour's fences. All three fences to the left of Robert's house had wooden nails and pieces of cloth here and there, but the fourth neighbour's fence had metal nails. From there on, each of the next five houses used metal instead of wood. She made the same discovery running in the opposite direction from Robert's house. The closest homes to Robert's used wooden pins, whilst the houses further away used metal.

As she returned to Robert's house, a thought struck her like lightning. She ran back inside and looked through the clues and the rest of the house in glances. Both Khendric and Topper watched her questioningly.

"Something is missing in this entire house," she said. "That ruby bugged me beyond belief! Why would someone leave a ruby like that, but go to the trouble of removing the ring? Someone left a wooden mixing bowl, which at first seemed like a coincidence to me, but I don't think it is. The sheath was left, but not the dagger." She paused, excitement bubbling inside her and waited for them to catch up.

"So?" Khendric asked.

"There is absolutely no metal in this house!" she said. She told them about her discovery with the fence.

"Hmm," Khendric hummed, rubbing his chin. He went to the front door of the house and grabbed the handle. "It's made of wood." He leaned down to inspect it. "Poorly made. It barely fits the hole. I didn't even think about it when we arrived. Topper, can you check the neighbours' doors?"

"Yeah," Topper said. "But look here." He pointed at the hinges. "They're made out of wood with a thin, smooth leather strap for sliding the door."

"What in the stonepudder?" Khendric said.

"We've got to check the neighbours," Ara said.

After a quick examination, both neighbours' brick houses had doors with metal handles and hinges. "Hmm," Khendric hummed. "We need to ask Robert if he ever used metal nails in the fence. And if he also had a metal handle and hinges, which he most likely did. If so, your theory has weight behind it. I have heard of a kind of snake that is believed to eat some alloys of metal but in this case, food has been stolen, and I don't think the snake would eat a dagger or replace nails with wood."

Ara still hoped she was on to something though and couldn't wait to ask Robert.

"And I seriously doubt we're dealing with a doombringer," Topper said.

"Definitely not," Khendric agreed. "Though a doombringer would explain the missing steel, the whole town would have disintegrated by now."

"What's a doombringer?" Ara asked.

"I'll show you in the book later tonight," Khendric assured her.

"I have to say. I don't have too many suggestions for what we're dealing with," Topper confessed.

"Neither do I," Khendric said.

If they have no clue, what can it possibly be? Ara thought.

They walked back to the inn and found Robert still sleeping in the beast hunters' room. They woke him, and he scrambled off the couch, trying to compose himself. "What?" he exclaimed. "Is everything okay?"

"We just have one simple question," Khendric said, as Robert rubbed his eyes, yawning. "What did you use to build your fence? More specifically, what kind of nails did you use?"

"Huh?"

"I know it sounds strange," Ara added. "But we need to know."

"I used regular nails, of course," Robert answered, confused.

"Made of metal?" she asked.

"Yes."

"And the handle on your front door was made of metal?"

"Yes, it still is."

"No, it isn't," Khendric said. "It's made of wood."

"Nonsense," Robert protested. "I would have noticed if it was suddenly made of wood."

"But you didn't," Khendric said. "I didn't even think twice about it. And that means someone, or something, has indeed removed the nails from the fence and all the metal from the house," Khendric declared. "What on earth purposefully removes metal nails and replaces them with wooden ones, but also steals food, and other things made of metal? I've no idea."

"So, where do we go from here?" Ara asked.

Khendric stared at the floorboards, appearing to mull it over. Topper lay on the bed, eyes on the ceiling.

"We can go to Horana," Ara suggested. "Maybe she has some books or something to help us."

"She may be of use," Khendric mused. "Let's go."

CHAPTER 9

The First Culprit

Horana's library was grand. Ara had never seen this many books in her life. Shelves upon shelves with knowledge and not nearly enough time to get through it. When they arrived, Horana had led them through the secret Beast Hunter store, through her house, and finally to her library.

Horana had left them alone for now but promised to return with some other books she thought could be relevant.

That woman has too many books, Ara thought as she ran her index finger across the spines.

Topper flicked through *Dangerous Nox Plants*, while Khendric continued to look for reading material. The square library had four lounge chairs and a table, and several windows which let in the sun. The door opened and Horana entered carrying some books which she set on the table.

"Perhaps these can be of help?" she said. "We need to figure this out quickly. The people of Cornstead are getting anxious, you could say."

"We're finding more and more clues," Khendric said, picking up a book from the table. "But we're struggling on what to do next."

"There was another murder last night," Horana said.

"What?" Ara gasped.

"We haven't heard of it," Khendric said.

Topper put down the book he was reading.

"The authorities are trying to stop it from leaking out," Horana explained. "But they have their own problems too."

"What do you mean?" Khendric asked.

"I get information from different sources, and it appears the highest-ranking officer in this area, Mr Kontho, has died rather unexpectedly. I believe it has created chaos within the authorities. I don't know who has emerged as the new leader, but I fear secrecy is not a good sign."

"We have to stop these spores quickly," Khendric said. "Before more people die."

"Soon, the villagers will need someone to blame," Horana said.

"Have you figured anything out?" Ara asked her.

Horana shook her head. Something moved behind her shoulder. A shape slithered through the door and Ara reeled backwards in shock. A snake-like creature with several legs and a beak instead of a mouth, skittered across the floor and climbed onto Topper's chair.

"Oh, sorry," Horana said as the beast crawled onto Topper's lap. He seemed as calm as always. "That's Lance, our pet inuana."

"He's cute," Topper said, petting its scaly head.

"It's friendly?" Ara asked, still leaning against the bookshelf.

"Oh yeah," Horana said. "He only eats insects."

"I'm guessing he's here because we're reading books," Khendric said.

"Why?" Ara asked.

Lance the inuana tucked itself on Topper's lap and closed its eyes, seeming to sleep.

"Inuanas aren't common pets," Khendric said. "But not unheard of either. The reason he's in here is because they seek out concentrating people. We don't know why, but they love relaxing next to people who are concentrating on something."

"Oh," Ara said, walking closer to the inuana. It didn't open its eyes or stir. It had two holes on its small head, which she guessed were ears. It breathed heavily, probably sleeping deeply, its scales changing from grey to green the length of its elongated body.

"I'm sorry," Horana said. "I should have warned you."

"No, no, it's fine," Ara said. "I've just never seen one before."

"Thanks for the books," Khendric said, taking a seat. "We'll get to reading."

"I'll join you," Horana said, sitting down herself.

Ara studied Lance some more, discovering there were no nails on his many toes. He had eight legs, four at the front and four at the back of his body, and his scales were soft to touch. After Topper stroked him, she reached out to try herself, and Lance didn't seem to mind. He breathed so slowly that Ara was about to alert them he'd stopped when he inhaled deeply.

Ara grabbed the last book from the table called, *When the Culprit isn't Human,* and skimmed through the pages. She found nothing about spores, and after an hour or two, she was through. Sighing heavily, she rose to find a new book. Khendric had changed books multiple times.

I'm glad he's so efficient, she thought, as it potentially meant less reading for her.

Topper seemed so focused, his eyes drilling into the book. No wonder Lance was relaxed in his lap.

She tried several different books but found nothing about spores. Then she spotted one named *The Plant Life of Avania and Its Uses.*

There must be something in here.

There was plenty of information about spores, but nothing that matched what was going on in Cornstead. She leaned back in the chair and released a great sigh.

Khendric chuckled. "I know," he said. "It's truly boring."

As she flicked through books four and five, she still found nothing. Hours passed and her eyelids grew heavy. She picked up another book Horana had placed on the table.

"*Religious Fanatical Beasts?*" Ara asked, getting Horana's attention.

"We're getting nowhere reading the obvious ones," she said. "And I'm sick of reading about plants."

"Me too," Ara said. "Thanks."

The book opened with tales of the Mirewind people, who weren't really beasts. The early chapters produced nothing of interest. In one of the later chapters, however, was something that Ara thought might help the case. It wouldn't help the case with the spores, but rather, Robert's case.

Dwarves and their fanatical beliefs.

Though dwarves are extremely rare, they are worth mentioning because of their ever-strong beliefs in the dwarven god Khorin: The Warrior of the Afterlife.

Dwarves always travel in groups of five or six. They have a broad build and are packed with muscles, which are concealed under heaps of self-made armour. All members of a dwarven group are smiths, constantly striving to craft better armour and weapons. It's believed the armour and weapons are rarely used for combat, but rather a display of craftsmanship and wealth. This behaviour most likely stems from their religion. There's not a great deal of information in existence regarding their beliefs of Khorin, but it's assumed he was a great blacksmith.

Most dwarves live in mines and mountains, but some turn their noses towards populated areas or forests. They're not known to attack humans and are hard to spot in the wild. They're quite primitive, if the blacksmith-aspect is excluded. They eat moss, bark, insects, and animals. Their religion is taught mouth to mouth, as they don't have a written language, which is why there is believed to be many versions of Khorin.

Why should dwarves be worth mentioning if they seldom attack humans, and hide when we're near? It is because of one ritual called 'Khorin's blessed'. This is the ritual that makes them dangerous, and they practice it in whatever city or village they enter. To a dwarf, forging armour and weapons is their life task, and the art is held in higher esteem than anything else. To keep crafting, they need metal.

The group choose a worthy sacrifice, an individual they deem worthy of fighting with Khorin on the battlefields of death. The dwarves believe this a great honour and treat the chosen with a twisted kind of reverence. To the dwarves, this ritual justifies the plundering of the chosen's possessions, especially all the metal he or she owns. They're expert thieves and, despite their broad build, are agile and unbelievably quiet. They'll sneak into the chosen's house at night and steal various items, usually beginning with small items the victim won't miss. As time progresses, more dwarves enter each night until eventually, all things metal will mysteriously vanish.

They use the stolen metal to craft armour and weapons, but one crucial part of the ritual remains—the chosen is paid back by being accepted by Khorin, referred to as 'the sacrifice'. When the house of the chosen is empty of metal, the dwarves abduct their chosen and bring them to their hideout where they create an impressive feast which they deem worthy a dwarven god.

Before or during the feast, the dwarves forge a set of armour called 'the molten armour'. This is the armour they give to the chosen as thanks for his metal, and they believe he will bring it with him to the afterlife, wearing it while fighting alongside Khorin. The armour must be 'a part' of the chosen one when they are accepted by Khorin, which is why the armour must be molten. The armour will meld into the chosen's skin, starting with the greaves and ending with the helmet. The chosen must be alive when beginning the ritual and might die while being clad in the sweltering armour. If the chosen survives long enough for the helmet to be placed upon the head, this final piece of the armour will surely kill them.

The dwarven hideout is often close to the chosen's house. It will be a cave or burrow, buried into hills or underground. The dwarves do their smelting during the night, so the smoke doesn't arouse suspicion. The cave ends in a large room that contains various smelting equipment such as a forge and anvil, and a table for eating.

"Guys!" Ara screamed, getting their attention and waking Lance. "It's dwarves!"

"What?" Khendric asked.

"Dwarves! They've been stealing Robert's stuff—the nails, the ruby-less ring, the doorhandle, the dagger! That's why there were different strands of hair, because dwarves have different hair colours! And they're going to take him!"

"Let me read the book," said Khendric.

She tossed the book to Khendric who caught it easily.

Khendric read it aloud, and when he finished he looked horrified. "We have to find Robert, right now."

Horana had barely risen from the chair before all three of them exited the room. They found the Beast Hunter store and stormed through it, opening the door to the outside—where several constables surrounded the building. Ara came to a halt. Topper crashed into her.

"Stop!" yelled a constable. "You are under arrest."

"For what?" Ara asked.

"Don't move," said another, as three of them moved closer, batons in hand.

Ara had no time to think before they tackled her to the ground. She fought to break free, but it was too late.

"No! Please! We have to save Robert!"

Her hands were cuffed behind her back, Topper next to her, but Khendric was nowhere to be seen.

"Where's the other one?" a slimy, familiar voice asked.

Ara's heart pounded in her chest. She craned her neck to get a better look, her eyes falling on Officer Martyn, the constable from the morgue.

The constables surged into the Beast Hunter store until only Martyn was left outside with them. Topper strained against his cuffs, but his flesh would yield faster than the metal.

Officer Martyn knelt next to Ara. "I'm onto your game, darkora. It ends tonight."

"She's not a darkora," Topper said. "We're—"

"Silence!" Officer Martyn snapped, striking Topper's back with his baton.

Ara shrieked, and Topper groaned in pain.

"Stop!" she begged. "We need to save—"

"Shut up. I'm going to save Cornstead from you."

Martyn rose to his feet. A smile adorned his face as the brutish work of his constables reached them from inside the building, destroying the shop in search for Khendric.

"Finally," Martyn said. "We'll put an end to your facade."

CHAPTER 10

A Meeting with the Gallows

The cells were cold and poorly lit, the air damp. Occasionally, a tear ran down her cheek, but the heaviest crying was over. Ara rested her head against the rock wall behind her. No matter how much time passed, her heart and her breathing wouldn't calm. Her fingers wouldn't stop shaking.

Topper was in the next cell, separated by the stone wall. "This is terrible," he said. "We have to find Robert."

What if the dwarves were about to abduct him, and they couldn't save him because of the constables? Had they solved this piece of the puzzle, only to fail to save Robert?

"Are they going to kill us?" she finally dared to ask. The question had been running through her mind for hours, but her brain wouldn't let her form the words, too afraid of the answer. Her question echoed through the empty cells. They were all alone. Perhaps there were other sections of the prison with more cells, where other criminals were locked up.

"I don't know," Topper said. "But if so, I will take all the blame."

"What?" she asked. "No, I—"

"Ara, listen to me. If they, for some screwed up reason, want our lives, I'll take all the blame."

"I can't let you—"

"Yes, you can." Topper swallowed hard. "Trust me, it will all be okay."

"No, I can't—"

"Promise me, Ara!"

She had never heard him this stern before, his words bouncing back and forth between the prison walls.

"Trust me when I say, it's going to be okay."

"How can it be?" she asked.

Khendric and Topper had changed her life in a way she had never believed possible. They had given her the chance to find herself again, to piece herself back together, proving there was always hope, even in the darkest of times. Her life after Alena's death wasn't a life worth living. Yet from the mud that had been her life, a flower had blossomed the day they saved her from the rura. It flourished tall, stretching toward the sun—oblivious to the coming wind. It howled and she struggled to stay rooted. She wiped away the seemingly eternal tears.

"Topper," she said through her sobs. "What if this is it?"

"What do you mean?"

"What if this was all the time we had together? And now comes the end."

"Stop, what are you talking about?" He lowered his voice. "Khendric is still out there."

She leaned forward, elbows on her knees, and rested her face in her palms. "He can't break into a prison, Topper, and he has probably gone to save Robert from the dwarves."

No answer.

"Just let me take all the blame if so," he finally said.

"I can't do that."

"Listen, Ara," he said. It sounded as though he had moved closer to the bars. "There's something I have to tell you."

"What?"

"There's a reason you must put the blame on me."

A heavy metal door opened and the noise rang loudly through the cells. Several sets of footsteps approached. Four constables stopped in front of their cells, with Officer Martyn in the middle. His sickening smile put fear into Ara's heart, her stomach felt like it was full of squirming eels. He approached Topper's cell.

"Finally," he said. "There will be justice for the innocent people of Cornstead."

"What are you talking about?" Topper asked.

"Don't be coy with me, boy. I know what you've been up to. Mr Kontho couldn't see it, but I did."

"We're trying to prevent any more murders from happening," Ara said.

In a flash, he stood in front of her cell. "I know."

"You do?" she asked, perplexed.

"I've figured out your scheme. You're the villain, playing the hero. Disgusting, and it ends tonight."

"I don't know what you're talking about," Ara said.

"She had nothing to do with it," Topper said. "That's why she's confused."

Officer Martyn's brows furrowed and he stepped closer to Topper's cell. "So you admit it?"

Topper's breathing was heavy, yet consistent. "Yes."

"Thank you. Very noble, even for your kind."

Stunned, Ara couldn't speak. She couldn't let him do this. He was as innocent as she was, and Officer Martyn needed to free them so they could save Robert.

Officer Martyn gestured two guards to Topper's cell. They unlocked it and grabbed Topper, walking him out of the cell. He didn't resist. They escorted him away, and the sound of the heavy metal door rung again. Officer Martyn stayed put, watching them recede along the corridor.

"What are you going to do with him?" Ara asked.

"I'll show you," he answered.

Officer Martyn unlocked her cell door and grabbed her arm. She tried to struggle free, but he slapped her. Terrible memories of her father's beatings surfaced in her mind, bringing back all the pain and misery he had caused. It didn't ignite a great anger in her, but instead reminded her of the hopelessness she used to feel.

Officer Martyn dragged her through the metal door, and into the hallways of the prison. She didn't fight him. She couldn't fight anything. She hadn't changed with Khendric and Topper. It had all been a beautiful lie, a comfortable mask to wear, for had she truly changed, she wouldn't allow him to control her like this.

They entered a grand office with a large desk and a wide red rug. Behind the desk, three tall windows showed Ara that night had arrived. Officer Martyn walked her around the desk and sat her roughly down in the chair. He took a pair of handcuffs from his belt and cuffed her to it.

"You're making a mistake," she said quietly.

"Oh please." Martyn scoffed turning to the window. "You're not fooling me. I know you work with them, and when we find Khendric, it's all over." Ara felt a stab of anxiety in her stomach. "We should have arrested you before you entered the Beast Hunter store."

"Did you follow us?" she asked.

"No, you made it even easier. We had a lookout stationed at the store who alerted us when you arrived. Catching rats is easy. I'm afraid, Ara, your time is drawing near. I recently discovered proof of your dark arts, and I will expose you to the public. I'll tell them all how you poisoned the villagers with a dark substance to bend them to your will. You see, I stuck a piece of cloth up the murderers' nostrils after learning the trick from the mortician, and guess what I found in both corpses?"

Spores, she thought. *And he thinks I did it?*

"I found the dark material you're using to turn these good villagers into monsters, and it stops tonight!"

"You're insane!" Ara yelled, yanking her chain, her hopelessness finally turning to anger. "I didn't do that!"

"Once again, you don't fool me, and soon you'll no longer fool the people, either."

"What motive would I have? Why would I commit such gruesome acts against good people?"

"I've never known a darkora to need reason for their heinous acts," Martyn said, opening the window. "Though it's obvious, I must admit it took some time to figure out. The three of you come into town. You start corrupting people until enough die for Mayor Bragor to notice. He seeks the help of beast hunters, since, according to you, us regular constables are not able to handle the task. The two beast hunters come in to save the day for a big prize. Then you ride to the next village and perform the same circus act there. Luckily, I'm in charge now, and your fraud stops here."

"That's ridiculous," Ara said. "The murders started before we arrived. We're trying to help you! You need our help!"

Martyn swivelled and slapped her lightning-quick, but she gritted her teeth. She wouldn't be accused of these lies by such a small man. She refused to let her mind carry her back to those dark places her father had taken her. It was enough. Her despair transformed to fury. She lifted her head and stared defiantly into his eyes.

Martyn turned back to the window. "We do not *need* your help. You think you're so great, but you're not. Who knows how long you've been hiding inside our walls, corrupting our people with your dark arts?"

"This is personal," she said, remembering his distaste toward beast hunters the first time they met, and Nadam's words. "You don't even believe what you're saying."

Martyn glanced at her over his shoulder, hatred in his eyes.

"You want us to be evil. You *need* us to be. Because if not, it means you've been wrong about beast hunters your whole life."

Martyn took a step closer and stared at her, his jaw clenched, but Ara refused to look away. She met his dark, malevolent eyes, refusing to yield. He grabbed the armrests on her chair and dragged her to the window. "Look. Can you see it?"

A large crowd had gathered outside the prison. Multiple braziers burned in the night around a large wooden contraption with a staircase.

"Can you see it?" Martyn whispered into her ear.

Her breath caught when she did. A masked man tied a rope to the gallows with a trapdoor underneath. She froze, unable to wrench her eyes away from the noose.

"Ah, yes, you do. Soon, your lifeless body will dangle for days at the end of that rope. Soon, Cornstead will have its vengeance for what you've done."

He's going to hang me? But I've done nothing wrong. I'm not guilty.

"First, you will watch as I hang your dear beast hunter." Martyn turned her toward him. "And then, when you're as scared as you've ever been, I will put the noose around your pale neck, and you will suffer the same fate."

She trembled with fear. "No! Please. . . I haven't done anything wrong." Tears streaked her cheeks, and she sank into the chair, wretched and filled with despair.

"You've done too much," Martyn said. He shut the window, locked it, and walked away.

"Please!"

"Your tears don't fool me. Now, I have a man to hang. You're next."

He shut the door and left her to stare at her impending doom. The tears wouldn't stop, the fear overwhelming. Her hands wouldn't stop shaking.

The crowd outside grew, all there to see wrongful justice taking place. They all believed she was evil, and that threatened to break her. She'd endured too much evil and pain in her life to be associated with it now. She would not sit back and let it happen.

She rose from the chair and tried to pull free from the cuffs restraining her arms. They wouldn't budge and there was nothing on the desk that would be of any help. *Perhaps I can break the armrest off?* She tugged with all her strength, but to no avail.

The door to the office burst open, revealing three constables. They were imposingly tall and walked toward her without uttering a word.

"No!" she screamed. "Don't!"

They held her steady as one unlocked the cuffs.

"Please," she begged. "I'm not—"

A constable shoved a black hood over her head and they carried her away. She fought and struggled, but she was no match for them.

"Stop! Please! I'm innocent. You're being lied to."

The constables didn't put her down until she felt the night's cold wind on her body. They held her fast. Lights danced through the fabric of the hood. She was close to the gallows. *No, no, no. This can't be right. This can't be how it ends.* She'd been happier lately than she had in a long time and yearned to get back to investigating with Khendric and Topper. How her life had changed for the better made this all so much worse. Was this some sort of cruel joke? Lift her spirits so that when her unjust death finally arrived, it hit so much harder?

The hood was pulled off. She stood a short distance from the gallows' steps, rain hitting her face. Once more, her eyes were glued to the noose. A perimeter of constables separated her from the massive, chattering crowd. Two constables stood either side of her, one mighty hand on each shoulder, with the prison wall behind them. Her line of sight broke as another person was led toward the gallows—Topper. Two constables carried him up the stairs, hood on, closely followed by Martyn.

Her heart pounded in her chest, and she was drenched in sweat. As Topper drew the crowd's attention, the chattering lowered. The constables turned as well, all wanting to get a look at the action.

"Tonight marks the end of the recent murders!" Martyn shouted as he took his stage. "The end begins with the death of *this* man. . . this *beast hunter*!" He pulled off Topper's hood, revealing a gag in his mouth. His hair was chaotic and a bruise had been left by someone on his left cheek.

People in the crowd turned questioningly to each other. The words 'beast hunter' echoed like a wave through the masses.

"You see," Martyn continued. "They have played you for fools! Toyed with your lives!" Martyn waved a torch around for dramatic effect. The constables walked Topper onto the trapdoor. He looked brave and angry, even with the cloth sticking out of his mouth.

"They came to this village," shouted Martyn, "spreading their disease! They corrupted our minds, turned us against each other! Good people have murdered good people, our fellow villagers!"

The speech energised the audience. Shouting voices demanded Topper's death, and Ara's heart pounded harder and harder. *He's going to die, and I'm next.* The noose hung in front of Topper's face as Martyn paraded around.

"They brought a darkora to our village," Martyn continued. "She is the one who corrupted our minds, only to have the beast hunters save us from this supposed 'beast'!

When we have executed this beast hunter, we will do the same to the darkora!"

Her face paled as the blood drained from it. She grew lightheaded and was about to faint, but strong hands held her tightly, and she managed to remain standing.

The people grew wild, sucking up every word Martyn said. Ara had never been this scared, surrounded by a crowd of several hundred people all chanting for her death.

Martyn quieted, staring into Topper's eyes. He grabbed the noose and placed it over Topper's head.

Ara's breath caught in her throat. The crowd was transfixed, even the constables. *Perhaps I can escape*—one hand on her shoulder disappeared for a brief moment. Before she could move, it was back, though it didn't hold her as tightly as before.

Martyn removed Topper's gag. "Any last words?" he asked. But last words were useless now. The crowd was so riled up and aggressive from Martyn's speech, they wouldn't believe anything Topper said.

Helplessness and despair gripped Ara, almost buckling her knees. *He is going to die,* she realised.

Topper said something inaudible to Martyn. Martyn clenched his jaw in anger and gestured to the executioner. Ara froze, and a phantom pain travelled through her body as the executioner placed his hand on the lever.

The trapdoor released and Topper plummeted towards the ground. The gruesome moment slowed, his dark hair not following the fall at first, his clothes waiting to be dragged down by his young body, his eyes open in fear, and his mouth gaping with a scream. With a snap, the rope stopped, and Topper hung dead at its end.

The crowd roared—both hands on Ara's shoulders disappeared and she barely heard a grunt. Turning her head, she saw one constable sat against the wall, unconscious. The other grabbed her and violently dragged her back into the prison. Not of her own volition, she suddenly found herself on the floor of a hallway. The cheers rung through the door until the constable kicked it closed behind them.

"Get up," he said, removing his hat to reveal—

"Khendric?" Her mind could barely comprehend everything that had happened in the last ten seconds.

Khendric grabbed her and lifted her to her feet. "Come on. We have to move." He held her hand and guided her through the hallway, through a door, up a level, and to a window in an office. Her surroundings blurred with their speed. Khendric gestured for her to jump out of the window while he removed the constable's uniform which he quickly replaced onto another unconscious constable who was slouched on a chair.

"Khendric," she said, her voice cracking. "They. . . k—killed him."

He held her arms and looked into her eyes. "I know. I'm sorry."

A commotion from somewhere inside the prison reached their ears.

"We have to go right now," he said. "It's not far."

"But Topper—"

"I know, but we have to go right now."

He gave her a nudge, but her legs wouldn't move. *Topper is dead. He is no more.*

Khendric took her in his arms and lifted her. The commotion came closer. "Ara, you need to focus. I'm dropping you in two. . . one."

She snapped back to reality as gravity took hold of her, dragging her to the dark ground below. She barely had time to react before hitting the grass. Khendric followed, somehow managing to close the window on his way down.

"Come on," he said. "Run!" He dragged her along until her legs moved by themselves despite her numbness. They finally came to a stop in someone's backyard, breathing hard.

Khendric sat her down on a bench leaning against the wall of the small house. No light emanated from the windows.

"Are you okay?" he asked between breaths.

"You. . . saved me."

"Yeah."

"But why?" she wondered.

"What do you mean?"

"Why not Topper?"

He bit his lip for a moment. "I had to wait until everyone was distracted. Which was. . . when the lever was pulled."

"You could have saved us both," she said. "You should have saved him!"

He stepped closer. "Ara, not so loud."

"He's your apprentice," she said, her mind spinning in circles. "He's your long-time friend. You should have saved him."

Khendric gazed around the corner again. "We need to move. I see lights."

"I'm just some girl, but you sacrificed him."

"We need to check on Robert," he said, motioning for her to stand.

"Robert?" she said, anger lacing her voice. "Topper is dead and you're thinking about Robert."

He sat down, meeting her eyes. "Ara," he said, his voice mellow. "I'm so sorry, but you need to trust me when I say: it's going to be alright."

"How can this be alright?" she said, her voice hardening.

"We have to go. Robert wasn't at the inn. I've been there to check, so we have to get to his house." Khendric moved, dragging her along.

"Horana was right about you," Ara said, tears streaking her cheeks. "She said to be careful around you, because you change apprentices all the time."

Khendric grabbed her harshly. "Ara, this is not the time. Trust me. I tried, but I had no chance to save both of you. If I could have, I would. Now, move."

Her knees wouldn't carry her, shaking from fear and anger.

Not you, Topper, she thought. *I thought you couldn't die.*

In this darkest moment, she realised something. Ara had believed that Khendric and Topper were some kind of immortal heroes who killed monstrous beasts—but they were only men. As she took one last look through the crowd at Topper's dangling body, she told herself yet again: *They're only men.*

CHAPTER 11
The Search for Robert

Khendric dragged Ara to Robert's house. She was physically and mentally exhausted but tried to resist him every step of the way. She'd even lost both her shoes somehow.

He let him die. He let Topper hang to save me. The thought repeated itself over and over in her head, until the words finally found their way to her lips in a whisper. "You. . . you let him die."

Khendric held her in his arms. "I couldn't save you both, and I don't have time to explain. Ara, the streets aren't safe, and Martyn's men will be looking for you. You have to come with me."

Though she heard the words, it prompted no reaction.

"Did you even try to save us both?" she said, tears creeping back again.

"Ara!" Khendric thundered. "Listen to me very carefully. Believe me when I say, we don't have time for this! I suspect Robert has been abducted, and if we don't help him, the dwarves will sacrifice him. I have no idea when, but the sooner we find him, the better. They must be somewhere in this small forest."

She pictured that poor, old, scared man. How he'd come asking for help, with nothing left. Topper was dead, and she would have to deal with that, but if there was still a chance to save Robert, she should try.

"Okay," she said. "We have to save Robert, you're right."

"Now back on your feet and help me find him."

They jumped the fence and ran into the forest, slipping on the wet grass. There wasn't much light, but after some time, her vision adapted, and she could make out more details.

"Don't you have any paratis serum?" she asked.

"No," he answered, not slowing his pace. "I used it all." Tree-roots and small plants riddled the ground. "Look for somewhere they might have built a small cave entrance."

They came to a slight hill and ran upwards. Not long after, Ara faintly smelled smoke.

"You smell that?" Khendric asked. He was a few feet higher up on the hill. She nodded. "We're getting closer."

As she ran up the hill, the smell became stronger.

They searched the hillside, stopping by a large oak where the pungent smoke enveloped them. Ara inspected the tree and found a hole in the trunk about the size of her hand. She sniffed it, and it tickled her throat making her cough.

"I think the smoke is coming from this tree."

Khendric examined the hole, squinting slightly. "I think you're right. They've hollowed out the trunk and built a tunnel for their forge."

"So we clog it," Ara suggested.

Khendric ran his fingers through his black hair and rubbed at the back of his neck. "No, we can't do that with Robert still inside. I think the dwarves can tackle the smoke a lot better than he can."

Ara couldn't look at him without feeling anger. She turned away. *Stay focused.* Her hands were shaking; her legs felt like they could give out at any moment. The terrible memory of Topper dangling above the ground haunted her.

"They must have an entrance below," Khendric said. "Come on." They walked back down the grassy hill, searching for the assumed entrance. "It's most likely well concealed."

Ara rustled some bushes in hopes of discovering something, but it felt like trying to find a strand of real hair in a wig. After searching through more bushes and behind stones, the helplessness got to her. She sat down, leaning her back on a rock. This was the worst night of her life, even worse than the night her parents died. Her life had just begun to make sense, and finally she had felt like she was doing something she wanted to do.

The grass beneath her feet was strangely warmer than the rest. She put her hand on the spot—it *was* hotter. Her fingers frantically ran over the patch until she found a ledge to grab onto. With what remained of her strength, she lifted, revealing a round metal door. Peeking down, she saw nothing. It was completely dark.

"Khendric!" she said.

Moments later, he appeared beside her. "Amazing! This must be their entrance. I think you should stay here. It could get dangerous," Khendric said.

Without waiting for a response he went through the narrow door, vanishing into complete darkness. If it hadn't been for all the complaints he made, he would have been impossible to locate.

Wait here? He's telling me to wait here after all this?

Ara put her feet in the hole and lowered herself down into it. The tunnel was narrow, and she had to sit down and push herself onwards, feet first. She suppressed her natural fear of the dark and crawled deeper inside until she kicked against something leathery.

"Ara, what are you doing?" Khendric asked from in front of her.

"What do you think?"

"Get back outside," he snapped.

Ara exhaled sharply. "No."

"I'm not joking."

"I'm *not* going back outside. I am as much a part of this as you are."

"This is not the time—"

"So stop wasting time. You can't keep me from following anyway unless you come back up with me."

There was a moment of silence before Khendric let out an exasperated breath. "When did you become so stubborn?" Khendric resumed crawling and Ara followed as best she could. "This will get dangerous," he added.

"The worst that can happen is that I die, and you get to say, 'I told you it would be dangerous' to my corpse." Khendric chuckled softly.

After crawling about twenty feet, weak light made its way into the tunnel, meaning Khendric had crawled all the way through. She continued until she felt a dirt-ledge with her toes and ended up dangling her legs over the side.

"Don't worry," Khendric's voice came from somewhere close. "It's not far down."

Ara landed feet first. They were in a larger part of the tunnel, where she could almost stand upright. She brushed herself off. A faint light came from further down the tunnel but Ara could scarcely make out her surroundings. In front of her, Khendric took off his coat and placed it on a crate. Piles of boxes were stacked against the tunnel wall and there was a shelf with various kinds of food on it.

Khendric tried to open a crate, but they were nailed shut. He sharply turned his head, facing down the tunnel.

"What?" she asked. Then she faintly heard it. Metal hitting metal.

Clank. Clank. Clank.

A perfect rhythm from further down the hallway.

"What is that?" Ara asked.

"Sounds like a dwarf smithing," Khendric said, not turning from the noise. She remembered how the book mentioned their blacksmithing skills. "I'm guessing we're hearing one crafting something right now."

They followed the slightly curved tunnel. It was riddled with open crates and shelves, revealing different pieces of armour. Khendric took a pair of braces and attached them to his belt. "These are probably worth a lot."

Ara also fumbled inside a crate and found a round piece of metal, a tiny medallion attached to a dog collar with some letters carved into it. It was difficult to make out, but Ara was pretty sure it said Dala.

A new tunnel shot out to their left. Ara pocketed the piece of metal as Khendric peeked around the corner before leaning back towards her.

"It's just a short tunnel, but there's a metal door at the end. That's where the light is coming from."

A door? Underground? Ara thought. She peeked her head around the corner—there was indeed a metal door only a few feet away. She walked towards it and saw that the door was made from three equal, rectangle-shaped parts which looked to be foldable. The light came from a small square window on the uppermost part of the door. It wasn't tall. Ara could easily see through the pane. What was on the other side though, made her jaw drop.

There was a wooden table, surrounded by small, sturdy, broad men.

It was dwarves all along. I can't believe we were right.

She counted six, all clad in beautiful armour, each one different from the others. She waved Khendric over and he peered through and gasped.

"Those are actually dwarves," he said, eyes wide open in disbelief.

"You've never seen one before?" she asked, surprised.

"I think they were more prevalent before. We have to write about them in the red book. . . *if* we survive."

"Are they dangerous?" Ara asked. They retreated from the pane.

"I don't know," he answered. "They're all wearing armour, but the book didn't say they would attack a human if their lair was infiltrated. It did say they shy away from humans, but even a scared dog in a corner will lash out."

Ara looked back into the room. They were feasting. There were mounds of food on the table, which they tore into. Some of them had long beards—red, white, or black, stained with coal and smoke. It was difficult to see their faces, but they looked to have broad facial features, large noses and chins. The dwarf to the left of the table was taller and not as broad as the others. He appeared to be chained to the table. She narrowed her eyes, trying to get a better look and. . . *Oh no. . .*

"Khendric, it's Robert."

"By the stonepudders," he exclaimed, bewildered. "He's right there." Khendric ran his fingers through his thick, curly hair before holding his hand in front of his mouth. "I can't believe it. I was growing more and more certain he would be dead by now." Khendric smiled at her. "Well spotted."

Robert looked unharmed, except for being chained up. Next to him lay a bunch of armour pieces heating on a grill.

"That's the molten armour, right?" Ara asked.

"Yes, and we have to save him."

Ara leaned against the mud wall, thinking. "You can't fight all of them?"

"Though I appreciate your confidence in me, I don't think I can take on five armoured dwarves. The book said they rarely use the armour and weapons for combat, but even five clumsy dwarves, wearing armour, would be quite the task I think."

"Don't you have some kind of serum that makes you an incredible fighter?"

"No, I don't think that exists, sadly."

"What do we do then?"

Khendric slowly exhaled, seeming to think on it too, but something felt off. They frowned at each other.

"The hammering has stopped," Khendric said.

Ara stepped closer and peered around the corner. "I can't see... there isn't enough light."

"We should check it out," Khendric said. "Can't have some random dwarf sneaking up on us."

Ara nodded and peered through the pane. The dwarves were still eating frantically. "Let's go," she whispered.

They ventured along the curved tunnel, meeting more crates and shelves. It was impressive how many wares were down here.

Is this all Robert's? Ara wondered.

Just as the light was about to fade, another metal door revealed itself. It also looked foldable, but with no glass pane. Dim light streamed out from under it. Ara heard a voice from the other side of the door, but it was too muffled to make out the words. Khendric motioned for them to stop.

"What's our plan?" she whispered.

"I don't know. Wait until he comes out and... grab him. Maybe use him as leverage?" That didn't sound like an excellent plan, but she didn't have anything better. "We can't storm in there. We have no idea how large the room is, or where he, or they are."

They had no more time to plan as heavy footsteps approached the door. Ara's heart pounded and she had no idea what to do.

The muffled talk grew louder, and the door handle started moving from the other side. They both leaned against the wall and after a few seconds of struggle, the door opened. A bright red glow shone through the tunnel, illuminating the area in a blinding sheen. Ara's eyes shot open at the sudden exposure. She leaned harder against the wall.

"I hate these doors," the dwarf said, with a very distinct accent. It had thick r's and long o's. He wandered through the door, carrying a glowing hot piece of armour with a pair of pliers. He seemed oblivious to their presence. He had large ears with dark hair sprouting from them, and the same facial features as the others; a sturdy leather apron covered his torso, and he wore leather boots with blue linen trousers.

In a flash, Khendric kicked the dwarf's foot, making him stumble and drop his pliers. The molten helmet plummeted to the ground.

"No!" the dwarf exclaimed, but Khendric seized him around the neck, pulling him off balance. "What on the darkest..." the dwarf began, but Khendric silenced him with his hand.

"Stay calm," Khendric whispered in his ear. "Or you die." The dwarf didn't struggle, but Khendric kept a firm grip, nonetheless.

"You ruined it," the dwarf muttered. "Khorin's helmet. . . you've ruined it."

"Is there anyone else in the room?" Khendric asked Ara.

She darted inside the small hot room with the anvil and furnace. "No," she said.

"You've stained the helmet," the dwarf said.

"You have a man in here named Robert—ring any bells?" The dwarf didn't answer, still in shock from the loss of his handiwork. Khendric put a dagger against his neck. "Answer me."

The dwarf gathered his senses. "Yes, Khorin's chosen he is. . . and Khorin's chosen needs a flaggering helmet."

"We need to get him out of here," Khendric continued.

"Get him out?" the dwarf asked, confused. "But this is Khorin's night, and Robert is ready for the sacrifice. But now the helmet needs forging again."

It glowed brightly but was stained with dirt and buckled at the edges where it had hit the tunnel floor.

"You need to stay focused, dwarf," Khendric reminded him by softly pressing the dagger to his throat. "Robert will not be sacrificed to your dwarven god."

"Of course he will! He's chosen by Khorin and has eaten Khorin's meal. Khorin's meal is a gift from Khorin himself. To pay back, there must be—"

"No!" Khendric snapped. "Are your friends wearing weapons?"

"You don't seem to understand. Robert *wants* to be sacrificed. We asked him."

"So, Robert has agreed to be clad in molten red armour which will kill him?"

"What is it you don't understand? Yes, he wants to fight with Khorin on the fields of the afterlife. As will I when I grow old and the red armour awaits me."

"Are your friends carrying weapons?" Khendric repeated, pushing the dagger against the dwarf's skin. A drop of blood trailed down to his collarbone. He didn't react.

"Don't you know anything, you flaggerbean? It's Khorin's night, of course we aren't carrying weapons. Do you bring weaponry when performing Khorin's ritual?"

Ara was taken aback by the question. *Does he think we all believe in Khorin?*

"We don't sacrifice people," Khendric told him. "Not for any gods. . . or, well. . . some do but that's beside the point, you're not sacrificing Robert."

"He is ready and prepared, and we have taken his metal and used it ourselves. He must be sacrificed. He wants to be."

"Who wants to be put in molten armour?" Khendric asked.

"A true believer in Khorin. One who wants to fight with him by his side, on the eternal battlefields."

"Robert isn't a true believer."

"Yes, he is."

"How do you know?"

"It's simple. . . he told us."

"Out of curiosity," Ara said. "What would happen if he wasn't. . . a believer?"

"You don't know?" the dwarf asked. Ara shook her head. "Well, then we invoke the duel of Khorin, where an unbeliever must fight a believer. If the unbeliever isn't desired by Khorin, he would kill the believer, sending him to Khorin instead."

"So Robert would have to fight one of you if he didn't believe in Khorin?" Ara asked.

"Did you not listen?" the dwarf said impatiently. "Yes, that is right."

"Well of course he said he was a believer then," Khendric said. "He's old. He couldn't possibly fight one of you."

"He would never lie about believing in Khorin!" the dwarf said stubbornly.

"You dwarves are a special kind," Khendric said.

"When is he being sacrificed?" Ara asked, earning the dwarf's hard stare.

"After the feast, which should be done now. We're only missing the flaggering helmet." He gestured down to the helmet on the ground with his eyes. His teeth ground together as if something had shattered in him when the helmet hit the dirt. "Which we will have to reforge now, thanks to you."

"I think we're going to spare you that effort," Khendric said. "Now walk." He pushed him ahead.

Shadows danced on the walls of the tunnel as they stepped over the glowing armour, its light slowly fading.

"What's the plan?" Ara whispered, trying to make it inaudible to the dwarf.

"I didn't have time to make a plan. We'll just. . . have to give it our best shot."

"I don't like that," she said.

"Me neither."

As they neared the door leading to the feast, the dwarven voices grew louder, complaining about the helmet not being in place. Ara peeked through the pane while Khendric kept the dwarf at bay.

"They are disappointed with me," the dwarf said despairingly. "They will punish me for this."

"It's hardly your fault, dwarf," Khendric said dismissively.

"What do you mean? I didn't bring them the helmet."

"Because we stopped you. We obstructed you on your task."

"So? I still didn't bring the helmet."

"Shh," Ara said. "One of them is coming this way."

During Khendric and the dwarf's conversation, she had spotted the rest of the armour laying on top of a grill, heated by coal. They'd strapped Robert to some kind of metal table, raised diagonally. He looked paler than ever and beyond terrified.

"What are we going to do?" she asked, heart racing. "One of them is on his way to check right now."

"How long until he's at the door?" Khendric asked, positioning himself in front of the passageway. Ara ducked beneath the pane, leaning against the wall.

"In two–one–" she counted, and on beat, the metal door flung open, quickly followed by a loud BOOM!

CHAPTER 12
Quiet Conversations with Dwarves

Khendric fired his pistol. Ara's ears rang and the look on the dwarf's face told her enough—Khendric had shot and felled one of the dwarf's friends.

The dwarf turned red, and raised his fist to attack, but Khendric quickly pushed the dagger in his face and the dwarf reluctantly lowered his fist.

The ringing in her ears stopped and normal sounds returned. . . well, maybe not entirely normal. Dwarven screams filled the air mixed with the clattering of armour.

Khendric pushed the dwarf forward, calmly following him through the door. He tipped his head for Ara to follow. She entered, looking over his shoulder. The five dwarves aligned themselves in a half-circle around the door. To her right was the large metal grill holding the rest of Robert's molten armour. The feasting table stood in the middle with two dwarves on top, standing amidst a glorious assortment of food they must have stolen—chicken, potatoes, sausages, salads. To her left was the metal table where Robert was strapped, his wide eyes darting around the room.

Two dwarves gathered weapons from a rack. One held a large iron hammer and the other a two-handed sword.

"What's going on here?" one of the dwarves demanded.

"He killed Emmer," another shouted.

"I did. Terribly sorry about it though," Khendric said, not appearing sorry at all.

They all bore angry terrifying faces which scared Ara to the core. The only thing lending her strength was Khendric's confidence and nonchalance which helped bolster what little courage she had.

"Get him!" The dwarf closest to Khendric yelled and charged.

Khendric levelled his gun at him. "Hey! Hey! Hey! Slow down now!"

The dwarf stopped but didn't back away.

Khendric kept his gun aimed at him. "I am awfully sorry about killing your dear friend, Emmer. He was an unfortunate victim, but there need not be more bloodshed here tonight."

"What do you mean no more bloodshed?" the dwarf with the gun pointed at him said. "There is still more pouring out of Emmer!"

"Well. . ." Khendric began, dumbfounded by the remark. "I mean nobody else will have to die. It's a pretty common expression. I'm saying this can end with no more of you needing to die. I have a proposition for you."

It took a moment of uncomfortable silence until one of them answered.

"Yeah? Talk then!"

"That man over there." Khendric pointed at Robert. "You will release him and—"

The dwarves complained in unison, shouting all kinds of profanities regarding the importance of Khorin's sacrifice.

"See," the captured dwarf said to his peers. "He's completely insane."

"Algar?" The one with the hammer said. "Why are you in his grasp?"

"Well, I was carrying Robert's helmet when—"

"We don't have time for this," Khendric interrupted. "That man you have over there is not to be sacrificed!" The dwarves complained once more. "Silence! You will shut your mouths and let me finish."

"But," the dwarf with the hammer said. "We have smelted all his metal, and taken all his clothes, and eaten all his food. We must pay him back. He must be elevated to Khorin's battlefields."

"He doesn't believe in Khorin!" Ara shouted.

The room fell silent before one dwarf turned to Robert. "Is it true?"

Robert, still chained to the table, glanced back and forth between Khendric, Ara, and the dwarves. "Umm, well, yes I do."

"You see," the dwarf said, facing Ara. "He is a true believer, unlike you. And that's why you will never fight by his side."

"What a curse," Ara said sarcastically.

"I'm sure Robert will forgive you if you let him go," Khendric said.

"How can we let him live on with no possessions? That would be cruel. It's better to live beside Khorin, fight by his side. It's a great honour."

"I'm sure he would rather have his life," Khendric suggested.

The dwarves threw their hands in the air, as if Khendric was the moron.

"Can't you see how this is better?" The dwarf closest to Khendric said, gun still to his face.

"Ugh," Khendric muttered, exasperated. "Let me try one more time, and if *any* of you interrupt me, I will shoot you. Have we reached an understanding?"

Ara prayed that no dwarf interrupted him, holding onto the hope that this didn't have to get bloody.

The dwarves fell silent. Eventually a dwarf said, "Yes, get on with it then!"

"The deal is, we take Robert home with us. I will give him food, clothes, and everything else he needs, so you do not need to worry about him being without possessions. Then you'll leave Cornstead and go back up to the mountains from wherever you came, never to harm another human being again. Nobody else dies." No one answered. "Well?"

"There is one great problem with that," the one with the hammer said. "And that is our doom. Your way will doom us all!"

"How?" Khendric asked.

"If we don't sacrifice the chosen to Khorin, after we have done the smelting and used his wares, we're left with the greatest sin. We could never return to the mountains with that guilt, and most importantly, we'll never fight beside Khorin on the fields of the afterlife. Khorin demands this sacrifice!"

Khendric rolled his eyes. "I hate religious fanatics. I need your help fighting them, Ara."

"What?" she said alarmed.

Khendric fired his gun, killing the closest dwarf, before running the dagger into his captive's neck, blood spurting through the air. The dwarves grabbed their weapons. Khendric fired his gun again at an unarmed dwarf. The bullet ricocheted off the plate armour. The dwarf charged towards Khendric, who fired another shot, grazing the dwarf's cheek. He didn't even flinch, and Khendric readied his sword.

Instinctively, Ara ducked behind the table to hide. It seemed to work, because they were all focused on Khendric.

The dwarf threw a punch at him, which Khendric expertly ducked and jabbed the dagger under the dwarf's arm. He roared in pain, blood spurting. The next three dwarves stopped and seemed to consider, trying to circle

Khendric. The recently-stabbed dwarf fell to the ground and didn't move.

The dwarf with the hammer swung at Khendric, who ducked again and closed the distance between them. He disengaged before doing any damage—the broadsword coming down. Khendric spun to the side, delivering a quick kick to the unarmed dwarf's knee, throwing his balance off. He dodged the sword, which landed on the hammer's shaft, disarming that dwarf. As Khendric came around from his spin, a fist met his cheek—the dwarf who lost his hammer had reacted quickly. Khendric stumbled backward, and Ara realised she had to help.

What can I do? she thought. The dwarves rushed Khendric, and he only managed to stay in one piece because of his longer legs and speed.

They're all focused on him and I have no weapon.

She surveyed the room, quickly locking eyes on the massive stack of weapons. She ran over, ready to grab the first thing she laid her hands on. Even Khendric's sword looked like a toy compared to the battle hammers and great swords. Her fingers wrapped around a large mace, but as she lifted, the heavy weight made her stumble forward, crashing her nose against the rock wall; it didn't break, but her hands came away bloody when she rubbed it.

Countless clinks, clanks, and grunts reached her ears, as she prayed Khendric could keep three dwarves at bay. Beside the weapons rack she saw a hammer. She grabbed it and rushed toward the violent deadly fight in front of her.

The dwarves surrounded Khendric, which meant Ara had an open shot at a dwarven head. She struck the unarmed dwarf, the hammer head digging into flesh and bones—but the skull didn't crack. As her surprise attack failed, fear of losing what little control she had, culminated in her stomach. *What now?*

The dwarf barely stumbled forward and turned to face her, gritting his teeth in anger. "You flaggering fool!" he shouted and charged at her.

Ara slammed her hammer once more, but it bounced off his armour.

He collided with her and they fell backward onto the feasting table. The dwarf raised a dangerous fist. Ara reached for a plate, the food flying off as she lifted it in time. The dwarf's fist hammered the plate into her chest, absorbing most of the blow, though it still hurt.

She dug her hand into some kind of green cream and slapped it over the dwarf's face.

He immediately tried wiping it off, giving her enough time to kick herself further up the table, but not far enough before a hand latched into her thigh. The dwarf's face was still green but for one eye.

Ara smacked a plate of food into his face, meat and vegetables spilling onto the dirty floor.

Unfazed, the dwarf dragged her back under him and lifted his fist again—this time, Ara found a fork and stabbed it into the dwarf's underarm. He reeled back in pain, giving her a chance to get to her feet.

She kicked various plates of food at him, the salads sticking to his face. While he was occupied with cleaning his face, Ara rolled off the table and found the hammer. Khendric was struggling on the ground with a dwarf on top of him. Ara had an opportunity to strike at her closest adversary, but Khendric needed help too. She threw the hammer, praying for her aim to be true. Her eyes widened in disbelief when the hammer crashed into the back of the assailant's head and Khendric used that moment to cut the dwarf's throat.

Rapidly closing footsteps alerted Ara of an oncoming foe— and he was pissed off. She skirted around the table, buying her a moment to grab a knife. She threw it and it hit his face with the blunt side, a sinister smile slashing his face as he bent to pick it up.

"How dare you interrupt this holy evening!" he said, charging her.

Ara ran around the table again, but the dwarf climbed on to the bench and threw himself at her. His bodyweight was enough to crash her to the floor. They rolled until she ended up on top, but he pinned her down again and punched her stomach. Her insides felt like they were in her mouth with the blow, and with no control of the situation, the dwarf rolled them around. She lifted her hands to protect herself, but she could do little against the knife.

The dwarf's arm came down, the sharp edge aimed at her chest as a hand grabbed him from behind and turned him around, a sword stabbing through his neck. He fell limp, and Khendric dragged him off her—the handle of the knife protruding from Khendric's thigh.

"You—you've been stabbed," she stuttered, pointing at the wound.

"It's going to be fine. Don't worry about it. I'll deal with it soon."

"Are you... are you sure?"

Khendric shrugged. "I've been stabbed before. This isn't bad."

"You have?" His perfect skin said otherwise.

All the dwarves lay dead on the ground, blood oozing from their bodies.

"Are you okay?" he asked. "They hit hard, but I think so."

"I can't believe it," Robert's voice rang through the cave. "You did it. You saved me!"

"Luckily, we did," Khendric said. "And we'll get you out as soon as we find the keys."

Ara ruffled through the dead dwarves' pockets, which felt

peculiar and nauseating. They were dead, their lifeless eyes staring relentlessly ahead, when moments ago they had been alive, sinister, and cruel in some ways, but alive. She closed their eyes, as much for her own comfort as theirs and kept searching until her fingers wrapped around something that felt like a key.

"I got it," she said. She went to Robert and released him, and the old man hugged her.

"Thank you, thank you."

Ara sat down on the bench next to the table.

The room, previously the scene of a great feast, was now a terrible room of death. Metal and flesh mixed with dirt and blood, but at least the problem was taken care of... well, one of them at least.

"I was sure I was dead," Robert said, shivering. "The thought of being put in that molten armour, I've never been so scared in my whole life. These bastards are some real monsters. At least lying about believing in their god was easy. They believed me right away, no questions asked."

"Yeah. That was a nasty ritual indeed," Khendric said. "You should thank Ara, she's the one who discovered the culprits."

Robert walked over and sat down next to her. "I am so glad you're a part of their team. Where is that Topper fellow?"

Ara sighed, the vision of the gallows returning. "Topper is dead." She fought to keep the tears from starting again.

"What?" Robert said. He looked to Khendric, who wrapped a long piece of cloth around his wound. "Is it true?"

Khendric swallowed dryly. "Yes. I couldn't save both of them and—"

"Aren't you sad?" Ara interrupted him. "Why aren't you crying?"

Khendric looked away. "Robert, you should find all your belongings down here. I'll help you if it's safe for us. And after that, we'll all help ourselves to whatever we want down here. But first, I need a moment alone with Ara."

"I understand. I'm really sorry about Topper." Robert wandered out of the room toward the shelves.

Ara clenched her jaw. "Is it that you don't care? Do you even care about me?"

"Listen," he said softly. "I'm sorry. I care deeply about you. I care about Topper too."

"Those are just words."

"I risked my life to save you," he said. "I do care about you, Ara."

"And Topper?"

He looked away and sighed. "You're not going to feel happy about this, but I can only say that it's going to be alright. Trust me. I know it's not what you want right now but trust me."

She looked into his dark eyes, searching for answers which weren't there. This wasn't good enough. Those stupid answers weren't good enough. Khendric wasn't who she had thought him to be, and finally it showed. She kept her anger to herself, too exhausted to start screaming again. Containing her emotions was familiar, she'd done it all her life.

The night sky was still over Cornstead as they left the dwarven cave. The village was silent. Ara shivered from the cold and wondered if the constables were still searching for them. She hoped they were far away. She was overjoyed at having saved Robert's life, but angry it had come at such a high cost.

"It was terrible," Robert said as they walked towards his house. "Suddenly there were five small men in my room. They hogtied and carried me through the window and off to their cave."

"Luckily we got you out," Khendric said.

"Master Beast Hunter and Ara, thank you from the bottom of my old, wrinkled heart. When I heard the shot and saw you and Ara come through that door. . . at first, I didn't believe it." Robert shed a few tears. "I still can't believe that I'm alive. It's like a piece of me is still down in that cave waiting to be burned alive." He shuddered. "Well, thank you! I owe you everything I own."

Khendric chuckled, while Ara followed along silently. "You don't owe us anything. There are great sets of armour and weapons down in the cave, and probably a great deal of gold, judging by the golden embroidery on their armour. We'll see what we can find down there and then sell the wares; we're probably both looking at a very nice profit. And you should enjoy those treasures too."

Profit? He's thinking about profit? I've been wrong about him. Am I only the next apprentice until I've expired too?

"That's some compensation at least for almost being burned alive," Robert said. "As long as I find the heirlooms Morosel and I owned, and essentials for living, I'll be satisfied." He shook his head. "But of course I'm not foolish enough to turn down riches."

"That's the spirit," Khendric said.

As they approached the inn, they checked the area for constables but it looked clear.

"I'm going to climb into our room and throw down a rope," Khendric said.

They snuck close to the walls of the building and he climbed onto the roof using the adjacent building to push himself up. Carefully opening the window from the outside using a wire, Khendric entered, and shortly after, a rope fell toward them. Ara climbed first, and together, they hoisted Robert up. As they dragged Robert over the ledge, Ara sat down in pain—her stomach hurt tremendously from the blow.

"Are you okay?" Khendric asked.

After a few strained breaths, she said, "Yeah, I think so."

"Let me have a look." He lifted her shirt and revealed a blue bruise on her stomach. "You should get some bed-rest and let this heal."

"Thanks for the advice," she snapped without looking at him.

Khendric sighed and went to the closet. He dipped his face into a bucket of water and cleaned himself up, washing off the coal stains and dwarven blood.

"I'm going to have a chat with the innkeeper," Khendric said. "Even if I have to wake him."

"Why?" Ara asked.

"I need to convince him of our innocence. Robert, you must come too. You're a local. He'll believe you more than me, and plus we have this." He fished out a beautiful dwarven bracelet from his pocket. "So he'll know we're not lying." He looked at Ara. "You should go to bed."

"I will," she said, tired and exhausted. Her body yearned for sleep and food. She could eat tomorrow, but right now she wanted her bed.

Khendric and Robert went downstairs, and Ara went to her room, barely closing the door behind her before falling into her bed.

CHAPTER 13
Stealing Back Stolen Goods

Her mood over the next couple of days was sour. Ara stayed in bed to heal, which bored her beyond belief. All she had to occupy her was the red book of beasts. The first few days the pain had worsened, but now finally, on day five, she felt better.

The innkeeper had helped them after hearing Khendric and Robert's story, aided by the dwarven artefact. For being so kind, Khendric gifted him the bracelet. They had moved to new rooms in the cellar, small and void of natural light, but safer.

Ara had practically been alone, except for brief conversations with Khendric when he brought her meals. Their forced conversations were composed of strained niceties.

Days passed, and no constables had come to the inn searching for them. Khendric helped Robert move back into his house over a period of several days and nights, which meant he was gone a lot. He changed clothes often so as to not be recognised, and it had worked so far.

On Ara's fifth day, she could walk around without excruciating pain.

Khendric came to her room and smiled when she saw her on her feet.

"How is the outside world?" she asked.

"If you can walk, why don't you come see for yourself?" He cast a smile at her, which was tempting to return, but she refrained. "We can go to Robert's and I'll continue to help him, while you spend some time outside."

"I'd love that, and I have a question for him."

As usual, he wore clothes that were different to his regular attire, a blue silk shirt and black pants. He gave her a similar outfit, accompanied by a hat to help conceal her face.

She left her room wearing the new clothes and entered the cellar. Large kegs of ale and shelves of food occupied the dark room, a staircase leading up to the world above.

Khendric climbed the stairs easily. Ara felt a tiny sting in her stomach as she made slow progress. He waited for her at the top, and she suddenly remembered something.

"Is your leg okay?" she asked, reaching the top.

"What?" he asked.

"After the stab."

"Oh." He snapped his fingers. "Yeah, it's fine now."

"Already? I've been in bed for days from one punch, but you've been running around seemingly from day one?"

He gestured for her to walk ahead. "Well, the knife was small, it didn't hit anything vital, and I had it treated properly. It still stings, but I can manage the pain easily."

Something in his voice sounded a little off but she couldn't pinpoint exactly what.

"Why didn't you send someone to treat me?" she asked.

"Your injury is the kind that needs time," he said. "I enquired, of course, but the answer was that you just needed to relax. And how's the reading going?" he asked as they walked through the bar.

A few people sat at tables eating or conversing. Nobody paid any attention to them.

"It saved me from dying of boredom," she said. "Does every beast hunter have one of these books?"

"No," Khendric said as they left the inn. "It's special to me—to us. I mean, it's special. The only one of its kind."

"So not every official beast hunter gets one?"

He shook his head quickly and she thought he seemed a little nervous. "There are some great books out there with descriptions though."

"Almost every chapter is signed by someone named Alec," Ara said. "Who is he?"

"Follow me this way," Khendric said, completely ignoring her question. He glanced away but not before she saw tears welling behind his eyes. "This is a more concealed route to Robert's."

She followed him through alleys and wider streets. No constables barred their way, and they got no suspicious looks; the fact that Cornstead was a large village and they were wearing new clothes clearly worked in their favour.

They reached Robert's house, which had been completely transformed on the inside. Tables, chairs, full closets and cupboards, tools, plates, pillows, clothes, shoes, and a bunch of dwarven stuff, blew Ara away as she entered. This had been a demanding job. Khendric hadn't *just* left her to avoid her tough questions, he'd been working hard too.

"Where's Robert?" she asked.

"Probably in the cave, gathering more of his possessions, or grabbing some treasure."

Moments later, someone approached the house, and Robert opened the door carrying two bags. "Oh, you're back, and Ara is with you." A huge smile spread across his face. "How are you feeling?"

Robert had transformed. His hair was freshly cut, his beard trimmed, the wrinkles under his eyes had shrunk, and he wore nice clothes. The glow in his face spoke of hope and rebirth, and for the first time since Topper's death, she felt a warm feeling kindle inside her. They hadn't just saved him but brought him back from the brink of destruction.

"I'm better," she said, grinning. "As are you."

"I am," he said, dumping the bags on the floor. They sounded full of utensils. He hugged her, and she embraced him back.

"Thanks to you, I get to live out my days, and not as a poor man anymore."

"I'm glad." This was why she had wanted to solve the mystery. If Robert could come back from his troubles, then it gave her hope of outgrowing the scars of her life.

"Do you still have more stuff to get?" Khendric asked.

"A whole day's worth of stuff," he answered. "But only if you're up for it. You guys have done more than I could ever ask."

"I'm up for it," Khendric said. "Not sure Ara is."

"I want to try," she said. "But first, I want to ask you about the spores. Why weren't you affected?"

Robert shook his head. "I have wondered the same thing. Maybe I was just lucky."

"Or maybe not. I noticed—down in the dwarven cave—a crate with what I believe held your belongings. In it was a small piece of metal, which I think maybe came from a dog collar. It read—"

"Dala," Robert interrupted her, a wistful smile on his face.

"So you used to have a dog?" Ara asked.

"Yes, I got Dala after my wife died, and she helped a lot. I loved her."

"What happened?"

"One day, not long before you arrived actually, she stood by the door, completely motionless. I couldn't get her to move; she wouldn't eat or drink. I lifted her away after some time, to which she didn't object." Robert's eyes glistened. "She got so thin but still refused to eat. She wasn't herself, and I tried to force food down her throat, but it didn't work. She eventually died of starvation."

Ara had experienced great loss in her life and knew what Robert had been going through, so she knew there wasn't much she could say to comfort him.

"I think Dala saved your life," she said. "She absorbed the spores for you, making them lose some of their potency. You could still sniff them, but I'm betting you weren't in the house much because of the dwarves."

"You're right," he said.

"Males and females react differently to the spores," Ara continued. "Because she was female, she became docile, like I did, only I got a far weaker dose."

Robert produced a faint smile. "Somehow, it's a bit better to know she might have saved my life, instead of just wasting away. Thank you, Miss Beast Hunter."

"I'm not a beast hunter yet," Ara said. "But I am glad to know I might have helped in some way."

Ara and Khendric spent the rest of the day helping Robert. Much of the physical work hurt, but when it got too bad, she took a break. Labouring outside felt so good compared to hiding in the cramped cellar room. The work took her mind off Topper's death: a much-needed respite. Those moments she remembered how far she had come, and what she had achieved. Because of her, Robert walked by her side, telling stories of his childhood which even made her laugh.

As night arrived, they placed his final belongings in the house and said their goodbyes. Robert shed a last tear of gratitude, before closing the door. She might never see him again, but at least it was a happy ending for him. The day hadn't been great, but it had been the best one since Topper's death.

She and Khendric walked through the alleys he'd chosen to be the safest ones on their way back to the inn.

"We still have no idea what caused the black spores, do we?" she asked.

"Sadly, no," he said, putting his hands in his pockets. "But I think we'll be able to narrow down some potential houses where they might strike again."

They entered a larger street, devoid of people, as darkness covered the village. Many houses were alight inside, the glow from the windows lighting up the otherwise dark street.

"I've been studying a map, and I think I've found three houses we could survey. I've scouted them out and made some plans. I just need to make some traps for all three houses."

"Three?" Ara asked. "Why three?"

They neared a fountain, and instead of answering, Khendric pointed at a sign on the brick circle. "What's this?" he asked, frowning.

We shine a light for those who turn dark.
Those who are taken by the corruption.
Together we are stronger, together we will fight.
Together we will rid ourselves of the plague. . . the beast hunters.

Ara felt a stone sink in her stomach.

"Let's take another route back to the inn," Khendric said.

The back alleys didn't slow them down much, and before long they were at the inn. They walked down the outside stairs and Ara noticed someone coming in the opposite direction. They both turned.

A figure appeared from the darkness, broad, and of average height. It was a man with dark skin and short hair, carrying himself with confidence, wearing a brown coat, much like Khendric's usual attire.

The man walked directly towards them with a determined look. Khendric said nothing as he examined the stranger.

Ara felt her heartbeat quicken. *Who was this man?*

The slightest hint of a smirk appeared on the man's face, and their eyes met. He stopped a small distance away.

"I have heard," he began with a deep voice, "that a man with golden teeth should fear the shinies more than anyone rich."

Ara's jaw dropped, her eyes growing wider than ever before. "Is that. . . a saying?"

Khendric smiled broadly and embraced the stranger in a tight hug. "Oh, how I've missed those stupid sayings."

"Topper?" Ara squealed, her head spinning. "Is that. . . you?"

The two men released each other and the man faced her. "I'm so glad to see you're okay, Ara."

CHAPTER 14

Explanations

Ara couldn't believe it. Topper was back, though he looked nothing like himself. She'd never felt so confused and happy at the same time before. Ara sat on her small bed in the cellar room, Khendric and this tall dark man who claimed to be Topper, sitting opposite her.

"So," the man said. "I guess I should start."

"How. . . I mean, you don't look like Topper at all."

The man had short hair and a slim face, with a strong jaw. "I remember everything," he said. "Up until the executioner pulled the lever, the fall, and the snap of my neck or not my neck, but. . . anyway, that was me. I remember you discovering it was dwarves, and then the constables came and seized us."

Ara's jaw dropped, her eyes wide. "But Topper died. I saw you die! And you look nothing like him! Is this a sick joke?"

"No, I did die, but. . . how do I put this? I am not exactly human."

"What?"

"I am what Khendric would call a beast. More accurate, I'm a morgal."

"Morgal?" Ara asked, still not convinced.

"Yes, a morgal is. . . I'm a black heart buried in a metal container at a cemetery. When I die, my beating heart adopts a freshly-dead body buried nearby and I reawaken. How exactly I came into existence, I don't know, but a long time ago, I just woke up in a casket and escaped for the first time. I was confused but could hear a heartbeat no matter where I went, so I followed the sound until I found the heart. Something inside me knew it was mine, which was a weird experience since I also had a heart beating inside the body I had claimed. I replaced the heart and wandered into the world for the first time. I don't remember the first body I was in—it's quite some time ago—and the lack of worldly experience got me killed pretty quickly. Sometime later—or right after—I don't really know, I awoke again. After countless deaths and always waking up in the same graveyard, I learned how the world worked. I remember most of the stuff from my previous lives, and I know that the dark beating heart is my true heart. Once, I woke as a young blacksmith, and forged a metal container, which I placed the heart inside before I hid it."

Ara could not believe what she was hearing. She had never heard of a. . . morgal.

"What he says is true," Khendric said.

"But. . ." she started, some of the pieces beginning to fall into place. "That's why you didn't save him?"

Khendric nodded. "I could only save one of you and as far as I knew, you don't come back from the dead. Ara, I am so sorry I didn't say anything. It's been killing me these past days, but I knew Topper would want to tell you himself."

"I'm truly sorry I never told you before," Topper said.

"You should have told me."

"I know," he said, his head hanging low. "I was scared you'd freak out or that you'd think less of me."

"I would never do that," she said.

"I've heard that from too many to believe those words." Topper raised his head. "So, I chickened out, and hoped I'd never need to tell you especially if you were going to leave us in the future anyway."

Ara had no idea how to feel. She felt betrayed—but still relieved Topper was alive. She knew she wouldn't have reacted the way he feared, or would she? Even though he kept saying he was Topper, it didn't feel like she was talking to Topper.

"Your personality seems different as well," she said.

"I have wondered about that a lot." Topper leaned back, rubbing his chin. "I don't know if you noticed, but my personality was kind of bland, perhaps. I've never really developed my own personality since I seem to sort of bring a core piece of personality from the host body that I'm inhabiting. With my previous body, it was the nervousness. I think maybe that's the reason I've a hard time figuring out who I am. I honestly never know if my feelings belong to me or the previous owner."

"So, how does that work? The dying part?"

"After I die, I wake up in another body close to where my heart is. I don't know the range of the revival because to me it feels instant, though I often discover that a couple of days have passed, sometimes even months. I never reincarnate as an old person—I think it has to do with them having died from old age. It seems I only inhabit the bodies of those who died from unnatural causes or accidents, and the bodies must be freshly dead. I kind of live on with their lives, and I've run into people who recognise me as their son, father, cousin, and so on, and I'm probably the reason for a lot of scary stories that way. Personally, I don't have a family though."

"That hurts," Khendric said, giving a small chuckle.

"Apart from you," Topper said to Khendric who tipped his hat in response. "I've purposely placed my heart in a kingdom that doesn't bury their dead, they just leave them in a coffin on top of the earth. When I woke after being hanged, I was in this body. I stole a horse and some clothes before returning to Cornstead."

"Wow, this is insane," Ara said.

"I've never had a better partner," Khendric said. "One that I can just sacrifice whenever I need to or if he pisses me off too much. It's pretty handy."

"The dying part does hurt," Topper reminded him.

"Not for long." Khendric shrugged.

"Wait," Ara shot in. "So, how old are you?"

Topper looked towards the roof, thinking. "I think I am... somewhere around two hundred years old."

"What!" she shouted, not believing her ears. "So for two hundred years, you have lived as other people?"

"Yes. Only males for some reason though, so I am fairly certain that I *am* male, at least."

Ara's head was spinning. She was thrilled that Topper was alive, but not in the way she had expected. She tried to wrap her head around this new reality, to truly grasp what, and who, Topper was. It sounded like he didn't fully know himself.

"Maybe," she said, deep in thought. "Maybe if you haven't figured out who you are over the past two hundred years and you easily come across as bland, you might be just that—a bland guy. Maybe that *is* your personality."

Topper scoffed. "Well, that just sucks to hear."

"I am glad you're alive though," Ara said, making him smile broadly.

"As betrayals come and go, only the loyal and the faithful remain," he said.

There it was: the warmth in her stomach returned. It was a wonderful feeling to be in the room with both of them, something she thought would never happen again. She glanced from one to the other before she laughed, bringing wide smiles to Khendric and Topper's faces. Why she laughed, she did not know, but it had been an unusual few days and finally, her family was back together.

"So, where do we go from here?" Ara asked, the laughter fading.

"We'll make traps," Khendric said. He proceeded to fill them in on his plan. He showed them which three houses he suspected as potential for the next attacks based on the elusive beast's previously assumed pattern, and the traps he planned to place inside and around the properties. Spike-traps would launch a board—like a catapult—towards the window opening, triggered by a pressure plate placed on the floor right below the window.

"What are we going to do with the people who live there?" Ara asked.

"I have spoken with them already," Khendric said. "After a long discussion about how beast hunters aren't bad people, I bribed them with some beautiful dwarven artefacts."

"We'll also have to make it impossible to get into the house through any existing cracks," Topper added.

"What do we do after placing the traps?" Ara asked.

Khendric put his finger on the map, running it over the three houses. "Each of us will stay in one house and wait for the potential beast to enter. The traps might reveal the creature and if we're lucky, we'll kill it. If it doesn't, and it starts running around the house doing whatever this mystery beast does, we'll signal each other. I've found some pretty good hiding spots in all three houses.

"At these designated positions, I'll place a long thin fuse that leads to each house. At the end will be a small explosive charge. I don't think the blast will be audible to the other properties, and therefore, it should not alert the beast. Once warned, we will surround the house the alarm came from, and from there we'll just kind of gauge the situation."

On the map, he noted where the fuses were from house to house. "But, in case we should need more immediate assistance, I'll equip each of us with a pistol. The fuse is going to take some time to reach its explosive, so whoever has been alarmed will be able to sneak close. However, if anyone uses the gun, we will come running."

Ara considered the plan. She didn't like the idea of being alone but found no better solution. "I don't know how to use a pistol," she said.

"Few people do." He took the pistol from its holster. Intricate and beautiful lines ran across its surface and one round part, which Khendric pointed out. "This is where I load the bullets and as I shoot, this part rotates making it possible for me to shoot more than one bullet. I've heard some call this a revolver, but to me, it's just a better pistol. The ones I will give you only have one bullet and take forever to reload, but it's great for signalling the others to come running." He handed Ara the revolver. "It's pretty simple. You aim at something and pull the trigger. Aiming is the hard part, but we don't have time to train you. If you have to use the gun, try to hit the beast. We'll all be equipped with swords too."

Ara nodded—she had never used a sword either, but it felt better to have one than not.

"When do you want to do this?" she asked.

"As soon as possible. Tonight? Are you up to it?" Ara nodded. "You are tougher than you look," Khendric said.

She appreciated him saying so, because she felt tougher than before. She'd stood up to Officer Martyn, escaped constables, solved a mystery, fought dwarves, and saved a life. She could take on a beast, she was sure of it.

"Khendric?" she asked, remembering another gnawing question. "What's a darkora? Officer Martyn said he knew I was one, but I have no idea what it is."

"Ah, it's a logical leap, to be honest. Darkoras are humans who have been affected—or influenced by—a beast's dark magic and survived. A few of those people start to show signs of wielding a kind of dark magic themselves. A darkora can come to be from simple magic, from a witchtroll, or more complex creatures like an illusioner, for example."

"Illusioner?"

"Creatures that come alive when there's a full moon. If you ever see a blue spectral light sailing through the forest when there's a full moon, run. That's an illusioner, and if it penetrates your body, you're as good as dead. Once inside you, you'll see otherworldly, and unthinkable illusions. It tries to kill you with unimaginable fear until your heart gives out. If you survive its illusions long enough, you tire it out and it will leave you alone, but very few people do."

Her heart pounded just hearing about it. "That's terrifying."

"It is. Officer Martyn thought you were a darkora who influenced people's minds to make them murderous. It's common to believe a darkora is evil, simply because they use some sort of dark magic, but that doesn't mean the human's mind has darkened."

"I see how it could make sense," she said. "But that man would never believe anything else no matter the evidence."

Khendric got up and put his coat back on. "No, you're right. He needed it to be true, so the actual truth didn't matter to him."

They stilled for some moments. Officer Martyn's face flashed in Ara's mind, and she doubted she'd ever forget it.

"Alright, it's time to go, if you're sure you're ready?" Khendric said finally.

Ara nodded. "I am. The beast won't wait for us, so we better be there when it shows up."

He nodded to her. "I'm proud of you, for everything."

She inhaled, her chest expanding with a new joy. Those words had been her dream her entire life. Her parents had never said them to Ara or her sister.

"I've never heard those words before."

With a massive grin, he hugged her. She returned it, letting her tears flow. Topper joined in too.

CHAPTER 15
The Source of the Spores

The night was dark with no moon to cast light over the village. Heavy rain tapped on the cobblestones outside, and the wind rustled the curtains. The night was very much alive, making Ara understand why so many tales took place in the dark. She shivered thinking about it, as she waited for a beast to come to her.

Ara waited in a makeshift hiding place within a cupboard with a clear view of one of the windows. There was a second window, out of sight, and rigged with nails on the floor and walls. Khendric had installed slabs of wood outside the windows, which could be pulled and closed by ropes within arm's reach; the window would then shut as a small metal rod, nailed into the wood, would catch on a locking mechanism, trapping the beast inside the house.

Ara kept guard at one of the windows. She had been here for what seemed like hours; keeping awake was becoming difficult. Often, she caught herself bobbing her head, toeing the line somewhere between sleep and consciousness. The constant rain outside didn't exactly help—the monotony of the sound tugging her closer to the dark comfort of dreams.

Ara made sure the fuse was tied around her arm. The matches were in her pocket. That was how, should the situation arise, she would call Khendric and Topper over from where they were guarding their own designated houses. She checked that the pistol was in its holster around her thigh—it was. There was something powerful about holding a gun. There was one bullet in the chamber, that much she knew.

I wonder how Topper is feeling now, she thought. *Is he scared? Does he care that he might die again?*

It was becoming clear how advantageous it was to have Topper as a companion—having an expendable partner was useful in a multitude of scenarios.

During the long hours in the house, Ara had acclimatised to all the regular sounds in her surroundings, which was why she was able to make out a new one that didn't fit. The sound's origin was hard to place, but it sounded like it came from outside the window she had her eyes on.

With a kick of adrenaline, she shot up, examining the area around the window. It could be a phantom noise because she was tired, but she wasn't taking any chances. It was a slithering sound combined with the smacking lips of a person eating with his mouth open.

Was it getting louder? It was difficult to hear over the rain.

Something grabbed the windowsill. Ara narrowed her eyes, vaguely making out a small shape like a hand. Her heart pounded; she clutched the pistol. Another form lunged over the windowsill. Ara got a better look, and realised it wasn't hands but small tentacles.

What in all the world is this?

In a flash, two dark tentacles pulled themselves up onto the windowsill and a creature lunged into the darkness of the room making no sound as it landed but slithering as it moved across the floor. Ara was about to light the fuse but realised it would reveal her. Who knew how the monster would react.

The wet sound seemed to fill the room as the beast moved around.

What should I do? she thought, sweat dripping from her brow. A match was ready in her hand, and she continued to listen. *Will the fuse even survive the rain outside,* she wondered, realising now how poor Khendric's plan was.

Then she smelt it, a whiff of something familiar. . . the spores! Quickly, she pulled a handkerchief over her nose, and without a second thought, lit the fuse. The fuse flared like a beacon in the night, leaving the house through a tiny crack in the wall.

It went utterly silent.

You better be on your way, Khendric.

She dared to peer out into the room. She couldn't see anything. Was it just quiet or had the beast escaped already? The thought of that thing touching her made her shiver. For too long, she sat in silence and dread, waiting for something to happen.

Vague footsteps echoed through the heavy rain, and Ara felt a flood of relief. The beast must have heard them also because the slithering sound returned. It sounded frantic, and

Ara spotted it crawling towards the window. It looked like a ball of small tentacles of varying thickness.

I can't let it escape, she thought, pulling on the ropes, closing the windows and turning the room completely dark. She was trapped inside with it now. The footsteps were gone too. The beast made no sound and Ara had no idea what to do next. Leaving the cupboard, she clutched the gun and readied her sword before sneaking closer to the door.

Suddenly, the beast slithered across the floor, charging at Ara. On instinct, she levelled her pistol and fired. The bright muzzle flash outlined the room, providing a glance of the tentacled beast. Wood chips flew from the bullet's impact— in her haste and mounting panic, she had overshot the creature by several feet. Another crack split the air and Khendric stormed through the door, with his torch, pistol, and scarf over his mouth to protect against spores. He quickly slammed the exit closed behind him, and threw the torch to Ara, who dropped her spent gun to catch it.

"Get down!" Khendric roared and aimed the pistol at her. His voice was muffled, but the words were clear.

She ducked and he fired. The beast crawled on the wall, trying to slither upwards to the roof. The only sound she could hear was a loud ringing in her ears from the pistol shot. Khendric roughly pulled her up, making her lift the torch to provide light. His sword was raised and he ran to the wall and launched himself at the ceiling, jabbing his sword into the shadows cast by the flickering torch.

"Where's Topper?" Ara asked.

"Keeping guard!" Khendric shouted. "And ready in case it tries to flee."

The tentacled mass shot out from the beam, straight towards Khendric's face. He ducked his head to one side, barely avoiding the brush of tentacles. The beast latched on to the wall behind him. Khendric landed on the floor, swinging his sword in an erratic swipe that missed. The beast skittered away from the blade, honing in on less dangerous prey. In a flash of incredible speed, its multitude of legs propelled it across the room straight towards Ara.

"It has teeth!" Khendric yelled, his voice barely audible over the ringing in her ears. "Don't let it bite you!"

Ara frantically swung her torch at the hurtling mass. It slithered aside and jumped at her. Instinctively, she ducked, and it landed on the wall once more, turning and lunging across the distance in a blink and scaling her trousers. The cold sucking pull of the beast's tentacles crawling up her body was too much to bear. She tried fending it off with the torch, but the flames licked her trousers too, sending scorching pain up her body. The creature clung on.

"Stand still!" Khendric shouted, but she stumbled through the room, trying to wrestle it off, and in the process, dropped her torch. The beast crawled up her arm and it felt like slimy rubber.

The torch rolled to the window drapes, where bright flames sprouted up the walls, licking the ceiling. The light revealed the creature in all its horror. It had a misshapen lump of a body, with numerous overly large glistening tentacles. Embedded in the horror were two jet-black eyes and a jagged slash of a mouth. A needle-like object roughly punctured Ara's flesh from the underside of the beast. Ara screamed in pain. The monster suddenly exploded as a bullet penetrated it, shooting skin and entrails in all directions.

Smoke left the barrel of Khendric's pistol just a few feet away. "Are you okay?" He rushed over, inspecting her arm.

Blood pulsated from a deep wound on her upper forearm, a dark liquid seeping out and mixing with her blood. It smelled overwhelmingly like the spores. The dark liquid looked like some kind of thick black oil, and her hand was already darkening as the viscous liquid coursed through her veins. Her arm went numb as the blackness spread towards her shoulder.

"I can't move it!" she cried.

Khendric's eyes widened and for the first time she saw fear in his eyes. "Ara," he said, but her hearing was fading.

"Khen. . ." she slurred, falling to the floor, as everything went black.

CHAPTER 16

Ara's Nightmare

Ara didn't know where she was. Her surroundings were white: the floor, the ceiling, or was it the sky? On the ground in front of her spread a line of dark tendrils, veins slowly growing forth like vines.

How did I get here? This can't be real.

One longer vein ran between her feet. She turned and followed it with her eyes, jumping back as her eyes settled upon a large throne partially enveloped by darkness. Atop it sat an entity shrouded in swirling smoke and shadow. In her heart, Ara knew it was evil, she felt wickedness emanating from the figure. It sat completely still, only grey legs and forearms visible, the rest hidden behind a veil. An otherworldly black material made up the throne, with red lines slowly dancing across it. Something felt so wrong in this place. This entity represented death, despair, loneliness, and nothingness.

A terrible fear ran through Ara's body.

I have to get away.

She ran as fast as her legs would carry her away from this purely wicked presence. She didn't look back. She ran and ran but when exhaustion forced her to stop, she turned her head—she hadn't gone anywhere, the throne merely a short distance away. Feeling utterly powerless and confused, her hands trembled with fear. She felt trapped.

"What are you?" she screamed, praying for this feeling of great sadness to abate.

"Another soul for my harvest." The throne vibrated violently as a dark, sinister, and powerful voice rumbled through this forsaken place. Ara's chest trembled and she barely managed to breathe.

A tendril grew forth from the dark spot on the ground, swirling its way into the distance, changing everything around them from white to pale grey.

"I see a lot of darkness in you," said the entity atop the throne. "Yesssss... your FATHER!"

A black figure in the far distance moved towards her with great speed, but the figure's legs weren't moving, it was gliding. Ara recognised him instantly—her father. She raised her hands to protect her face, but he stopped right in front of her, his jaw tight and his hands clenched in fists.

"I thought of killing you, so many times."

Ara lowered her hands. "What?" she asked.

"It would have been so easy," he continued.

This wasn't her father; it couldn't be—he was dead.

Am I dead? she wondered with heavy fear in her heart.

Nobody believed in gods—that was for lunatics and fanatics. Asking about the afterlife was prohibited and thoughts of the forbidden question drove many to madness. Ara sometimes couldn't help it though, and often wondered what would happen when she died.

"I could have done it so many times," he went on. "I could have drowned you in the creek, and no one would have cared. Not one person wanted you alive." Her lips trembled. Fear, disappointment, shock, and betrayal ran rampant in her mind. It felt like her heart was going to break. "Your mother wanted me to do it. She begged me to drown you."

Ara looked into her father's face. His mouth curled down like it always did when he readied to beat her, and his eyes. . . he was enjoying this. His eyes were darker than before.

"That's not true," Ara protested with a sob, feeling loneliness and despair pulsating from the throne behind her.

"She wanted me to murder you." He leaned closer. "But I could not do that. You see, I needed you to run your little cart back and forth from the market. You were nothing more than a pack mule to me and even less to your mother. After all, you murdered the only thing we ever cared about. . . your sister!" He roared, his face warping into a viscous tar-like liquid, smelting like a candle next to an inferno. He screamed, the skin tearing around his mouth. With a sick gurgle from his throat, he spat a foul wad of dark tar onto her face. Her father transformed into the substance and snatched at her as his hands melted away. "YOU MURDERED US!" he bellowed, his mouth full of oil.

Ara stumbled backwards, trying to put distance between her and the oily figure, but she was being pulled closer by the sticky arms. A last scream came from the malformed monster as it became a puddle of thick oil on the ground.

Hands clasped her throat from behind, strangling her. They were fiercely strong. Ara was lifted violently backwards, struggling to draw breath. Her eyes ran wild in their sockets.

"It's all true," a familiar voice whispered in her ear—her mother's. "And now you're going to die."

Her mother snaked around Ara's right shoulder, leaned in, and kissed her on the mouth, spewing liquid from her nose, ears, and eyes. The liquid caught in Ara's mouth and she choked. Her mother disappeared and Ara threw herself on all fours, puking up the dark tar, desperately gasping for air. Her tears fell, mixing with snot and tar, the tears morphing with the black substance into an image of her sister.

"Alena?" she said.

Her fingers shook, blackness falling like raindrops as she touched the image. Alena's mouth opened wide, letting out a shriek so terrible Ara recoiled back. She tried protecting her ears, but the voice sliced right through her hands.

Then it stopped.

Numb, exhausted, and feeling a sadness deeper than she'd ever thought possible, she rose to her shaking feet. Her surroundings had changed drastically. No longer was she surrounded by white—it had turned murky. The dark tendrils on the ground had sprouted all around her, pulsating with her rampant heartbeat. They were like veins, making the terrain rugged, slowly creeping towards her. In the far distance, a storm rumbled, black skies swirling rapidly, thunder reaching her ears, cracking loudly. The tendril leading from the spot to the throne expanded, growing thicker.

"Yesssss," the dark voice vibrated from the entity sitting motionless on the throne.

Ara's knees buckled and she landed in the tar.

"Feed me those twisted, sinister thoughts. They are all around you, in everyone you meet."

She fell through the black sludge, into a violent ocean of thick black water. The waves were enormous, the skies above mighty with blood-red rain. She fought to stay afloat, but the waves attacked her from all directions, dragging her down. She swallowed water trying to take a breath. Something grabbed her leg and dragged her down so rapidly, the water rushing past her, into a seemingly endless abyss.

No, please, let this stop!

Everything stilled around her. A young girl floated in the water with her, dressed in rags. her skin blue and bloated. She slowly rotated revealing a face Ara recognised.

Alena! She swam for her, grabbing, and pulling her close.

The endless ocean disappeared. She lay on the grey floor next to the dark spot and dark throne. She cried, begging for this torture to end.

Where is this? What is going on?

Alena moved in her hands. Ara looked down, but instead of her sister there was a pack of black rats. She screamed and jumped up, the rats scurrying into the dark spot on the ground.

"Khendric?" she screamed. "Topper? Please, someone, save me!" She fell back on her knees, all her strength gone. She found a black mark on her arm where the tentacled beast had stung her.

There was the soft sound of a beating heart. It beat slowly, slower than it should. The storm grew louder, as gusts of strong wind washed over her.

"You hear that?" the being said, her body throbbing. "Your heart is dying. My blood courses through your veins."

She clenched her teeth together and tightened her body to withstand the shaking.

"To you it is venom. To you and to all humankind, I am the end."

"I'm alive then?" Ara questioned, daring to raise her chin. "This is all in my head."

"Nobody survives my blood," the entity said, the ground shaking. "You have met me before, you inhaled my sickness once. I have been inside you at another time."

The spores, she thought. The oppressive feeling weighed heavily on her heart.

"But you lived. It has made you resilient to my touch. Sadly, for you, it only means a slower death."

"Stop!" she shouted. She couldn't take it anymore. She just wanted it all to end.

The heartbeat slowed down, the dark veins turned to tentacles and crawled up her legs. Ara quickly tore at them.

"Ara?"

A few feet away stood her sister.

"Alena?" Ara said.

Alena smiled, holding her doll, and ran to Ara, falling into her embrace.

Ara clutched her, holding her tight, breathing in her familiar smell. "Alena, I'm so sorry. It was all my fault."

"It's okay," Alena said, face buried in her chest. "I love you, big sister."

"I love you t—"

A sound broke through the coming storm. Thunderous hooves on cobblestones in the far distance. Ara frantically scanned every direction. They grew louder but were nowhere in sight. She held Alena closer.

"It's okay, don't worry." The sound of charging horses grew louder and louder. "It's okay, I won't let them hurt you."

They were nowhere to be seen, but the noise was overwhelming, drowning out everything else. The invisible cavalry was so close. Ara tightened her arms around her little sister, wrapping her body around hers—but still nothing came.

Ara heard her own laboured breathing and the storm. She looked up, still seeing no charging horses.

Ara screamed as she looked at her trampled sister in her arms. Her face was twisted, her body crushed in multiple places, intestines gushing out from her splattered stomach. She hung lifeless in Ara's arms.

"No!" Ara wailed. "Please, no!"

Alena started melting like a wax candle, her face contorting. Ara fought to keep her together, but she slipped through her fingers.

"No-no-no, please," she begged. "I can't. . . I can't do this."

Two tentacles latched onto her ankles. She tried to fend them off, but they were too strong. They constricted her legs.

"No!" she said, fighting with all her remaining strength, but her weak fingers yielded to their grip. Exhaustion caught up with her and she crashed to the ground, panting desperately. The veins on her right arm expanded past her shoulder, up to her neck.

Blood ran from the armrests of the dark, relentless throne. The entity rose, darkness following in its wake.

I'm going to die here, she thought, shaking. *All alone in this terrible alien place. Where are you, Khendric? Topper?*

"Soon it will be over." She could vaguely hear the being's heavy footsteps walking towards her. "Your life will be mine, forever. The world will be better off without you. Nobody is going to mourn." She would cry if she could, but her body wasn't responding. "Not even your dear friends."

In front of the entity, another figure walked toward her in the fading world. It was now the deepest dark of night. The figure went down on one knee in front of her. *Khendric!* A glimmer of hope sprouted deep within her. He was in his usual trench coat and large round hat but bore a sinister smile. His eyes were not his own.

"Finally," he said. "We'll be rid of you."

What?

"You're a burden. I hate taking care of you. I curse the day you came into my life."

No, please, not you too.

"How you ever thought you were part of our team is ridiculous. We'd never care for a foolish girl like you. You're pathetic."

Ara let the tendrils consume her; nothing remained for her in this world.

"Ara," Khendric said kindly. She slowly opened her eyes. He radiated a warm glow. "Hold on."

The darkness behind his eyes was gone, replaced by his real eyes and smile, before he vanished into red smoke. He left a pool of blood where he kneeled—it stood out in the darkness, like the crimson moon at night. Ara felt the warmth coming off it. She didn't think she would ever feel something this good again. The pool of blood expanded towards Ara. It crawled against her cheek, down her neck, continuing gently down her body. It felt warm to the touch as it slowly covered her body.

The being, shrouded in darkness, now stepped in front of her blurry vision, tall and imposing.

"Give in," the entity said. "Now." But its feeling of omnipotence had faded, instead carrying a hint of desperation.

Khendric's blood flowed from the wellspring in the ground and into her mouth, forcing her to cough. Some of it travelled down her throat and tasted like iron. It was warm, and strangely refreshing.

Her head felt less groggy, her eyesight slowly regained its focus.

"What are you doing?" the evil entity said through the howling wind. Ara realised death wasn't coming for her at all. She was getting stronger. This blood was helping her body to heal. She sucked in more of the liquid.

Suddenly, her father and mother reappeared, looking into Ara's eyes.

"We can make it all work again, Ara," her mother said. "You can be our little girl again. You, me, your father, and Alena. Just like it used to be when all was good. All you need to do is stop fighting and before you know it. . . the four of us will be back at home."

A tear rolled off Ara's chin as her mother rested her head on her father's shoulder. They used to look like this. Happy and caring. It was so tempting—to have a real family and loving parents again. Alena, her sister, appeared too, falling into her father's arms. She was fine, as beautiful as the day she died. Ara wished this perfect family in front of her could be real.

"Come, join us, Ara," she said. "Let's be a family once more. A happy one."

Ara never thought she'd experience a happy family again. After her sister's death, she had longed for her parents to turn back to their former selves. But with every day that went by, hope withered, and slowly, Ara realised her parents would never be the same again.

She took a long look at them and treasured this false memory deeply, before sucking more of the blood from the ground. They disappeared, turning to dust in front of her eyes. The darkness slowly yielded. The tendrils constricting her body evaporated, and with them, she regained feeling in her extremities.

"You were mine, but you're just out of reach. What are you?" The entity faded out of existence as it too turned to dust, the gruesome vibrations abating with it.

Ara continued to drink. She could move her arms and feet freely again.

The darkness turned back to pure white light. The storm ended, and only the dark mark on her arm remained. She rose, understanding for the first time, with total clarity, that she had returned from the brink of death.

"You will never get rid of me," the voice whispered in her ear. "You have felt my touch, and you will never be truly free again."

CHAPTER 17
The Dark Veins

"Can you feel a pulse?" a deep voice spoke.

"I—I can. I can't believe it."

"Oh thank the stonepudders."

Everything was dark, but wherever she was, it smelled of iron, dirt, and food. Her back felt uncomfortable, as if laying on something hard.

"It worked," the first voice repeated. "It actually worked."

She recognised the voices. *Khendric and Topper?* Her eyes opened to two familiar faces.

"This is real, right?" she asked.

"Yes, this is real. Are you okay?" Khendric asked.

She was in the dwarven cave, laying on their feasting table, hence the smells.

"I don't know. What happened to me?"

"Remember that tentacled bastard in the house?" Khendric said. "It stung you, injecting some cruel venom into your bloodstream."

"I remember that," she said with a weak voice. "I woke up in some other world where everything gradually turned dark and. . . I had some horrible visions. There was something so evil in there, an entity that pulsated all kinds of negative and terrible emotions." Ara's eyes began to well up. "I never knew such evil existed. It hated me."

"I am so glad you're alive," Khendric said. He wiped away her tears.

"We thought we lost you. Your heart stopped for several seconds," Topper said.

"It did? But I'm alive? How?"

Khendric shot Topper a peculiar look. He cleared his throat. "We killed the beast. Cornstead is safe for now. How safe it is for us is an entirely different story. We burned that house to the ground and even if nobody saw us, I'm fairly certain the constables will pin it on us and deem beast hunters even more criminal than before."

"But we saved them!" Ara said. "There has to be a way to tell them."

"We could try, but it would be risky. They would need time to see that no new murders are happening before they'd believe us. It would be easy for them to conclude that you, the darkora, haven't been using your dark magic as of late and we'd be right back in their claws. I think it is best for us to leave."

But I've risked my life to save them, twice. She sighed heavily. "I want them to know that we helped them. They should know that beast hunters aren't evil."

"I do too," Khendric agreed. "But sometimes you have to let that thought go and be the evil monster they think you are."

"Well, that's unsatisfying," Ara said, crossing her arms. That was when she noticed dark veins running along the skin of her arm and all the way up to her neck.

"No! No-no-no!" she screamed, thrashing, falling off the table. Khendric grabbed her before she hit the ground.

"This isn't real! I'm still in there!" She looked in terror at her arm and the black veins. "No, no, please no."

"It's alright," Khendric said gently, holding her in his arms. "This is real. When the venom spread through your body, the veins in your arm turned black."

She breathed heavily. "If this is some cruel vision, I'm done."

"It isn't. This is real."

She glanced at her arm, disgusted at how it looked. Her throat had dried up, and she coughed. Topper handed her a mug of water.

She wrapped her fingers around the mug, and it broke in her hand, shattering like a wooden wall hit by a cannonball, water flying in all directions. Ara sat still, eyes wide.

"What was that?" she asked slowly. "Something is wrong with me!" Her breathing quickened. "I need to get out!" She grabbed her shirt, feeling strangled by it.

"Ara, please, calm down," Khendric said.

She rose to her feet, stumbling as she was still weak.

Khendric grabbed one arm and Topper took the other. "This is real," he said. "You're out of there!"

"How can I know?" she cried, attempting to break free of their hold.

They held her tight, but she fought to break free—and threw Topper across the table and into the wall. Khendric slapped her cheek hard. Shocked, she stopped fighting, turning to him with eyes wide open.

"I am very sorry," Khendric said. "But that did have its intended effect. Can you feel that pain? It is real."

Ara did what he said, running her fingers over her already-red cheek.

Topper composed himself and brushed dust off his shirt. "Don't ever tell anyone she literally threw me over a table."

"But how did I do that?" She studied the limb with carefully measured calm. "This is just like in the nightmare. It slowly grew up to my shoulder." Ara flexed her hand and arm a few times, examining the veins further. "It feels normal."

Khendric walked around to the other side of the bed and presented his hand. "Grab it and slowly apply pressure." She did, and before long Khendric yielded. "Stop! It's about to break."

"I'm sorry!" *Where had this strength come from?*

Topper gave her the metal ring that had been on the bottom of the mug. It was still a circle, completely intact. "Try this."

Ara took the small metal ring and, squeezed it. It crumbled in her hand.

"I think the venom has enhanced the strength in that arm," Khendric said slowly.

"Is it dangerous?" she asked, trying to keep the fresh memories of her nightmare at bay.

"I'm not sure." Khendric frowned. "We don't know what will happen to your arm. It might fade or it might be permanent."

"Did I do it by myself?" she asked. "You know, come back? I could feel my heartbeat weakening, but at the end you appeared." She pointed at Khendric. "Then the most peculiar thing happened: I drank your blood."

Khendric looked away, sighing heavily. When he gazed back into Ara's eyes, he bore a look of sadness. "To save your life, I gave you my blood." Khendric grabbed the transparent tube he'd used for the blood transfusion from the table and held it up for her to see. "Most likely it would've killed you, but you got lucky, and it healed you."

"What? Why did it heal me?"

"My blood has regenerative effects."

"What do you mean?"

"It means my body regenerates and heals itself a lot quicker than a normal person. We transferred my blood into your body, and luckily it healed you."

"Really?" Ara said in awe. Khendric nodded. "It all makes sense now, how your leg seemed fine so quickly after you were stabbed, while I took days to recover from a punch. How does your blood have this ability?"

Khendric's eyes displayed a deep sorrow, however. His lips quivered.

"Khendric?"

He nodded, though not convincingly. "Well, my parents, they. . ." Tears welled in the corners of his eyes.

Ara felt a peculiar prickle in her mind as Khendric tried to talk, like a faint pressure inside her skull.

"After the bandits came—"

"You know, few people survive his blood," Topper interrupted. "You could've died."

"Really?" Ara asked. She noticed Khendric's relief at Topper's interruption. Although she was curious to know more, clearly the past brought Khendric pain, and no one understood that more than she did. "But why did I live then?"

"We're not sure," Topper said. "The blood seems to heal some and kill others. We've tried it out on me several times over the years and I either healed or died. I carefully noted every attempt. Out of ten attempts, I died seven. But we had to risk it with you as it was our last resort."

Ara's eyes widened as she grasped just how lucky she had been.

"It's advantageous for us to know though," he added, "that you are compatible with his blood. If you get injured again, we'll use it to heal you."

Ara gave a half-smile. "That's pretty reassuring. We're a strange bunch, aren't we? You're not even human, Khendric heals himself, and I have a freakishly strong arm." Topper chuckled—Khendric remained stoic. "We're in the dwarven cave to hide, right?"

"Yeah," Khendric said, seeming to blink away tears. "The place is pretty handy for staying out of sight. Ara, I have to get out of here. I'm sorry for being brash about it. Talking about. . . my blood, it brings—"

"It's okay," she said, placing her arm on his. "I understand."

He nodded to Topper and went out the small door.

"Do you know what that's about?" she asked Topper.

He shook his head. "He's never told me anything. When we've broached the subject in the past, I tiptoe around it, or else he gets like this."

"Will he be okay?"

Topper shrugged. "He's always been okay in the past, though it takes him a couple of days usually."

She sighed, feeling terrible for causing him pain.

"Don't worry about it. We'd both rather have you alive."

"Thanks," she said, allowing a feeling of utter gratitude wash over her.

I'm alive, and I'm back with Khendric and Topper.

She'd been close to death, and felt its embrace, but she'd survived. The warm feeling in her stomach returned, and though she felt drained and exhausted, she was alive.

"So, what do we do now?" she asked.

"It's time to leave Cornstead, but first, you need to eat and sleep. Once you're feeling better, we'll go."

CHAPTER 18
The Beast Hunter of Cornstead

"You will be mine."

Ara woke abruptly, gasping for air. Sweat trickled from her forehead. The dwarven chamber was uncomfortably warm.

It was a nightmare—just a nightmare.

The large room was empty, though someone had set out clothes for her on the side of the bed. Her arm was still tainted with the dark veins running from her shoulder to her wrist.

Ara rose and put on the new outfit. It was a beautiful leather vest with a black shirt beneath. The vest was thick and sturdy and clung well to her body, fitting perfectly. The trousers were of comfortable wool—also black. Lastly was a brown cloak with a hood.

She walked to the door, not certain where to go, but she had to get out of there. She gripped the door handle and—

"Give me more blood," a voice said. Startled, she leapt back and scouted the room. She was still alone.

How can I know this is real? She remembered Khendric's slap and the pain. *That was real,* she told herself, running her hand across her cheek.

She once again placed her hand on the door handle and opened it—straight into Topper, who was so startled he yelped, stumbling backwards.

"You deserved that," she said, recovering from her shock.

"Why?"

"For sneaking up on a girl like that."

"I was coming to wake you! We're ready to leave."

"As you can see, I'm up and ready."

Topper examined her. "You like the clothes?"

Ara nodded eagerly. "I do."

"Good. I paid good for them."

"What did they cost?"

"Fifteen gold chips."

Ara gawped. She'd never held that much money. "How much do you have?"

"Not so much now," Topper answered. "We've bought supplies and clothes. The innkeeper has sold us much of his food since we 'saved the village', as he put it."

"Well, we *did* save it."

Topper brushed imaginary dirt off his light brown coat. She still wasn't accustomed to the new him. Talking to him felt like talking to Topper, but the way he acted and his mannerisms were completely different.

They came to the narrow tunnel leading out of the dwarven hideout. Ara was relieved to be active again. Though tired, she'd grown weary of sleeping and letting the world move on without her. Topper grabbed her shoulder. It was so weird, looking into those dark eyes. "Listen, Khendric won't be himself for some time. And I don't know how long it will take."

"I see," Ara said, feeling guilty.

They went through the narrow tunnel and reached the other end. The fresh air and light comfortable wind were like finally removing a bandage from around her head. She breathed in deeply. The sun was high in the sky, and the grass was as green as ever. She turned towards the tunnel.

"It feels good leaving this behind."

"I agree," Topper said. "Khendric is waiting with our horses at another gate on the eastern side of the village. We should make haste. He's most eager to get going."

They walked, and she felt peaceful at leaving the village.

Before long, they were out of the small forest. Topper led her through the streets that followed the city wall. Ara kept clenching her fist, feeling the awesome power of her enhanced hand.

After sneaking through the alleys and streets of Cornstead, she finally spotted a small stone gate far ahead. There was some traffic—a few horses and people walking in and out. The gateway did seem far busier than the one they entered when first arriving in Cornstead. A smile spread across her face recalling the thief posing as a guard—how ridiculous he had been. A lot had happened here, and in a way, she felt it had shaped her more than her seventeen years in Kalastra.

Topper rolled a hood up over his head. Ara did the same. He was dressed in black leather clothes, his outfit almost a replica of Ara's.

"Despite this gate being busier, it's further away from the prison, and there are generally less constables here. It will be easier to blend in due to the number of passers-by. The more people, the less chance of singling out two beast hunters and a young woman."

A little boy, no more than ten years old with a shaved head, was watching another boy talking heartily with a pretty girl. He was spying on them, the jealousy obvious. Passing him, Ara felt a weak ominous sensation in her mind, pulsating from the envious child.

What is going on? She rubbed her head.

They neared the gate, but Khendric was nowhere to be seen.

"He probably went outside already." Topper waved a hand for her to follow.

There were two constables posted at the gate, overseeing people coming and going. They seemed more interested in people entering the village, rather than those leaving, their backs turned to Ara and Topper. They passed the constables without being noticed and followed the road with the thinning crowd.

The road bent naturally into a forest, leading them away from the constable's line of sight. The forest wasn't thick but provided enough shelter.

"I hope Khendric isn't still in the village," Topper said.

Ara hadn't even considered that. Some sense or premonition, like a whispering itch at the base of her skull, told her he was up in the woods, behind a stone formation. A faint pulse pressed on her mind like before.

A sharp whistle sounded and Topper let out a sigh of relief. From behind the stones came Khendric holding the reins of all three horses, his hat pulled low to cover his eyes. He brought the horses down to Topper and Ara. She was happy to see him, but he didn't even look at her as he handed her the reins. He wore a sombre expression.

"How are you doing?" Topper asked.

"Fine," he snapped, climbing onto his horse.

"If you need to talk—"

"I'm fine." Khendric motioned his horse into movement.

Ara caught Topper's eyes and he shrugged.

Ara climbed on to Spotless, who seemed thrilled to finally leave the inn's stables. He'd been fed well too, gaining a little weight which he would lose now that they were back on the road. It felt like ages since she was last on him. Since she had seen him, she had fought dwarves and the tentacled beast, and solved the mystery in Cornstead. To think she might have been training to be a nurse and missed out on a life-changing adventure. She had been hurt, both mentally and physically, but it had only strengthened her and now she was ready to leave the place of her rebirth behind. It felt good.

Thank you, Cornstead. And thank you Khendric and Topper too, for giving me a chance.

She hoped Khendric would get better soon. Without his laughter and constant mocking of Topper, the mood was sombre.

They didn't go further into the forest, instead continuing on the dirt road out of Cornstead. Khendric led them, rocking back and forth in his saddle with a slumped posture. Ara hated that their easy conversation was gone. She rode Spotless further up so she was next to Khendric.

"How did you and Topper meet?" she asked.

"On a case," Khendric answered stiffly.

"Care to elaborate?"

"No."

"I will," Topper said. "It was on a case, and I was the beast. A woman claimed to have seen the dead come alive, and she was right. She showed Khendric the empty casket and he investigated. After some time he found me and we talked, or bonded, over some drinks. He asked if I wanted to join him, and to be honest I didn't have anything else, so I said yes."

Ara chuckled. "Are you serious?"

Topper nodded. "Yep. Best thing to have happened to me."

She hoped to see a reaction from Khendric, but there was none. He sat still in his saddle, seeming not to care about anything.

Cornstead disappeared behind them, and the forest was to their left with a vast plain to their right. It was like two different worlds, separated by the narrow road. As Ara shot the village one last glance, she noticed two other riders far behind, clad in black cloaks. She frowned, following them with her eyes. Hoping it was nothing, she turned back, but couldn't let the ominous feeling go from her mind—something felt wrong about them.

The road sloped slightly uphill, and at the top was a large tree. Under it, stood yet another rider. The sun made him look like a silhouette on his horse.

Two more men on horseback appeared on a small sideroad from the forest, trailing behind them. Her gut told her something was wrong. Topper noticed it too, giving Ara a nod. She looked to Khendric, but his stare was downward, hat covering his eyes. They neared the top of the hill, and Ara tugged at Khendric's coat, gesturing with her eyes at the cloaked men.

"Well, well!" a voice said. It was the rider in front of them, the voice familiar. "Trying to run away from the law?"

Officer Martyn.

Ara's stomach twisted inside out. Topper simmered with hatred, his eyes glaring intently at Officer Martyn. She hadn't seen Topper this angry before, and it was scary. Khendric halted his horse and they came to a stop behind him. The other horsemen circled them, their faces concealed behind hoods and scarves.

"You even set fire to a house before you fled, burning it to the ground."

"We did that to kill a beast!" Ara proclaimed.

Officer Martyn snorted. "Silence, darkora! Of course, you would claim to be killing a beast. An easy excuse to make when you fail at killing decent folk."

"Let us go now," Khendric said in a calm yet stern voice. "Or I will kill you all."

Officer Martyn laughed. Khendric slowly moved his hand towards his holster.

"Hold it right there!" Officer Martyn drew a crossbow from his belt. "I know how those things work. Don't you dare touch it." On his belt hung two sheaths, one containing a sword and the other a dagger. He had armed himself for battle.

Though Khendric's hat covered his eyes, Ara saw a faint grin forming.

Was he smiling at a time like this?

Ara felt a droplet of sweat travel down her forehead.

The other men unsheathed daggers. Ara waited for Khendric to say something clever like he usually did, but he remained silent which stressed her even more.

Focus. You need to stay calm.

Flexing the strong hand helped—her secret weapon. She quickly inspected Officer Martyn the way Khendric had done to the soldier when arriving at Cornstead.

"We have rid the village of beasts now," Topper said through gritted teeth.

Officer Martyn frowned. "And who are you?"

"Where is your constable's medallion? Your official uniform?" Ara asked. Officer Martyn's eyes lingered on her and his expression soured.

She wasn't certain about her assumption, but it was worth a try. "Why are these men not wearing constable clothes, instead wearing hoods and concealed daggers? This doesn't seem like the work of constables."

Hatred blossomed in his eyes. "There have been complications," he said, his thin lips barely moving.

"You're not a constable anymore, are you? That's why you're here, outside the village. You don't have any authority."

Officer Martyn flinched slightly. "Bah! That doesn't matter. The people will know I saved them, no matter what the new superior Jackon says. I will return a hero when I have your heads. The people are with me."

"He disagreed with you," Ara added. "Blaming the beast hunters was wrong, and he knew it."

"Stop it!" Officer Martyn said, waving her words away. "He is a fool, and I grow tired of talking." He levelled his crossbow and aimed it at Khendric's heart. Ara cried out as he released the arrow, but Khendric ducked faster than Ara had ever seen him move before, the arrow flying over his head, as he grasped his pistol.

In a flash she kicked Spotless into motion. The horse responded quickly and galloped towards Officer Martyn. A rider came into vision, trying to stab her with his dagger, but she leaned out of the way, and continued riding.

Multiple gunshots cracked through the air behind her from Khendric's direction, followed by metal hitting metal, but she rode on, focused on Officer Martyn.

Both horses reared to avoid a crash. Officer Martyn swung the crossbow at her, but she ducked and tightened her hand to a fist. For the first time, she summoned all her new strength and struck—her blow connecting with his shoulder.

He flew off his horse, spinning in the air, and crashing hard to the ground.

Ara dismounted Spotless with haste and ran around to find Officer Martyn squirming on the dirt road.

He unsheathed his dagger and lifted it towards her as she approached, but she caught his arm and clenched her fingers, forcing him to drop his weapon. Something crunched within his forearm. He screamed in pain, falling backwards, clutching his broken limb.

"Damn, darkora!" he said, gritting his teeth.

Ara's hands tightened around his throat. Surprised at the strength of her hold, his eyes grew wide.

Officer Martyn gasped for air. He tugged at her fingers, trying to remove Ara's mighty grasp. Ara turned back seeing Khendric shoot the last of the corrupt constables. Around him lay the other constables, unmoving, blood soiling the ground. Topper came up behind her while Officer Martyn struggled under her grasp, his face turning blue.

Topper went down on one knee and whispered to Officer Martyn, "I told you that killing me would change nothing for I would come back to see you dead in the ground long before your time is due."

Officer Martyn's eyes widened in horror as he realised who Topper was.

Topper rose and leaned close to Ara. "If you wish, I can be the one to end his life. We are against killing humans, except when it is necessary. This man is certainly a monster, and if you cannot finish him, I will gladly do it for you."

Ara considered his words. She wasn't the fragile girl she had once been. She relished the feeling of assisting the helpless, like Robert. She had also grown stronger; all the pain from her previous life had moulded her into someone else. Someone who could make difficult choices, like this one. What she held in her hand was not a man, but a monster... a beast.

Officer Martyn had murdered someone he knew was guilty of no crime and hung him in front of a crowd as an example of what would happen to those who defied him. That ended now.

Ara peered into his dark eyes. Her hands tightened, crushing his throat. The sounds were terrible, and blood gushed as his skin tore open. Ara forced herself to look at him until he finally stilled.

Khendric came up behind her. He put a hand on her shoulder and nodded respectfully.

"The Cornstead case ends with him," she said, proud that she had seen it through, and that she had killed the worst beast of all.

A comfortable, refreshing breeze rolled over her. Her world was not as it had once been, and she wondered what adventures lay at her feet next. Something told her that her journey with Khendric and Topper had only just begun.

BEASTIARY

Shinies

Known location: the known world.

Type: Small, non-lethal.

Weakness: General weaponry and traps.

Shinies are small creatures around the size of a grown man's hand. They're characterized by a flat horizontal beak and two little hands with eight fingers on each. They have a plump back-end with a small stump of a tail, supported by two legs, with six toes on each foot. Their fur is thick, rough, and short.

Shinies often operate in small groups and steal everything that shines, hence their name. It's unknown what happens to their stolen goods, but they're rarely seen again. Usually, they don't torment the same victim for long, unless they have an unusual amount of shiny items, like an unending stream of silver and gold chips.

Despite their tiny brains, they have a natural sense of stealth, barely making a sound before, during, or after a burglary. Their victims will usually notice items disappearing before they notice a shiny. A coin, a watch, some sort of valuable stone (ruby, sapphire, etc.) often satisfies them, but some tend to steal several items at once. This makes them easier to notice, as shiny objects usually cling together.

Rich people usually seek the advice of Beast Hunters to protect their wealth. A simple trap is all that is needed—one with a rope that wraps around the shiny's leg. To lure the shiny into the trap, display one shiny item that appears more valuable than any other. This basic trap can be made more complex with additions like poison to make sure valuables are not lost. The disadvantage with this kind of trap is that it makes it easier for common thieves to steal someone's most valuable possession.

The shiny should be killed to ward off its fellow accomplices. This has proved to be the most effective method to keep them away.

- Alec

Witchtrolls

Known location: Sangerian Grasslands and the kingdom of Bodera, the Mud-lands.

Type: Small, cunning, wields simple magic.

Weakness: General weapons, counter-magic if a darkora is available.

Witchtrolls are small, humanoid creatures, about the size of a hand. The population seems exclusively female. How they reproduce remains a mystery. Witchtrolls are considered quite intelligent and are well versed in trades like tailoring and wood carving. They tailor long robes for themselves and even small hats have been found. With their woodcarving skills, they craft small staves. Their skin is dark-green, and they are bipedal. Their fingers and toes have long nails, and many consider them ugly. Their faces are misshapen, with asymmetrical features and crooked noses. Their mouths are larger than what would seem natural, and they have few, but large teeth. Their eyes are yellow like a lizard's and they have a short tail. They don't seem to communicate in any specific language.

If spotted, it's ill-advised to let the witchtroll get away. They steal food and small personal belongings, eating the food, and using the items to perform rituals. It's generally believed they take pleasure in seeing misfortune strike innocent people. They use the owner's personal items to cast curses upon him or her, often resulting in bad luck or unfairness. The magic can influence the owner's mind or those around him, and the outcome is never desirable. Their charm is not strong, as they are small creatures and can in some cases be warned against with a simple negative-stone.

If left to their free will, witchtrolls will continue to curse the individual either until they get bored, or death occurs.

- Alec

Vengeful Remnant

Known location: Bound to no location.

Type: Ghost, spectral.

Weaknesses: Varies, and depends on the specifics of the case, though have typically been reported to attach to the buried bones of the dead, a treasured heirloom, or item of great importance. There have also been cases where the remnant is bound to something treasured by the victim, or in particularly unsavoury instances, specific body parts of the victim. Destruction of these artefacts will sever the connection between the vengeful remnant and the living realm.

A vengeful remnant is created in different ways, and the rules don't seem completely consistent. Usually, they're made from powerful emotions, like hatred or jealousy. This happens when a person is murdered or dies violently. To pinpoint exactly what kind of death— and uncover the relevant circumstances surrounding it— appears impossible, as the variations are great.

An example follows: One man loved his wife, but one day caught her cheating with the man's brother. The woman killed her husband, and the extreme betrayal, and jealousy at the time of death, turned him into a vengeful remnant. This is one of many stereotypical scenarios known to create these vile beings.

The vengeful remnant haunts the person who caused the extreme emotions, manifesting in different ways. It starts with nightmares, items missing, or objects suddenly falling over. As time goes by, the behaviour becomes more erratic. It can behave in many ways: mirrors breaking when the haunted victim looks into it, cutlery levitating, or even visions of the dead. As the haunting progresses, the remnant becomes stronger, and more aggressive. This can take days, months, or even years. The remnant reveals itself in dreams or in real life to the victim, and sometimes attacks. These attacks can leave scratches and bruises. The vengeful remnant's attacks vary from physical to mental terror, both deadly.

Burning the bones of the apparition has proven to remove it in most cases, but it's no guarantee. If burning the bones doesn't work, try to find an object of importance to the remnant or the haunted victim. Destroy this item. Morbid as it may seem, if the vengeful remnant murders its victim, it will disappear by itself.

- Alec

Mire Woman

Known location: All kingdoms, but only in mires.

Type: Unknown

Weakness: Unknown

These beasts have earned their name due to their behaviour, as no one knows their appearance. To best explain it, please read the following scenario: A young man travels along a muddy road on a misty night. To his left is a swamp. Through the night a woman screams for help, and he hastily paces towards the sound. Slowly, a female figure becomes slightly visible through the fog, uttering phrases like: "Help, I'm stuck", "Save me, I am about to die", or simply "Help!" She always has an appealing shape. The young man gets off his horse and walks towards the young, beautiful maiden.

After a few steps, just as the woman becomes clearer, the young man begins to sink into the ground. There are no known cases where anyone has survived beyond this point. By this stage, the woman is revealed to be a tangle of thorns and vines, formed into the shape of a woman.

As the man sinks, his bones fracture as the mire woman engulfs him. As his spine breaks, entrails often push through the body and out of the mouth, muffling his screams. His bones continue to break, until he is submerged by the swamp. This information was obtained during the arguably unethical experiments of the late 'mad' queen of Neira. She commanded one of her footmen towards the mist, having an observer note down the proceedings. No one knows what's hiding in the depths of the mire, but it's sinister indeed.

- Alec

Gremlik

Known location: Most capital cities and some villages past a certain population.

Type: Critter, medium size.

Weaknesses: General weapons, fire. Perfume seems to annoy them.

Gremliks are small, humanoid, dark-green creatures with long nails on their hands and feet. They have two long ears and two smaller ones resting lower on the skull. Exactly why they have four ears is unknown, as their hearing doesn't seem enhanced.

Their teeth are large and often in poor condition. The eyes are yellow, and, more often than not, one is lazy. Having a lazy eye gives them the appearance of being confused and is distracting. They have a large jaw with tusks.

Gremliks are the size of a human leg and have a bulky body shape. A gremlik wears whatever it can find and are often blamed when clothes left out to dry go missing. It's not unusual for gremliks to wear human clothes, fur, dead animals, trash, or even armour if they find any.

A gremlik will show itself to a human, mostly at night and when the human is alone, begging for food. They're trying to appeal to our sympathetic side and want something to eat. Be careful. Given too much food, the gremlik will stay in the area and come back for more.

If this is allowed to proceed, the gremlik will become angry and attack when not given any more, as their appetite only grows. One way to deal with these aggressive gremliks is to spray your whole house, yard, and belongings, with a strong perfume. The better the smell for humans, the worse for gremliks.

Given too little food, it becomes angry which can have dire consequences. Another well-used tactic is to scare the creatures away. Gremliks measure their enemies in size and if a larger opponent charges at them they will, in most cases, flee. It's also advised to bring a weapon, as they recognise it as dangerous. It's important to understand that when charging a gremlik, be ready to potentially kill it. Don't stop midway, revealing your bluff. Try to injure them in the charge as well, as that will diminish the chance of them coming back, seeking revenge, which they have done in a few cases.

The amount of food to give varies, but somewhere around two slices of bread and a small piece of meat seems to both satisfy and piss them off enough to leave one alone. An angered gremlik is dangerous, and they lash out in different ways, according to their personality. They are as strong as a rabid hound. Some gremliks will attack with murder as intent. Others might scream and terrorise to get their food, and some will even harm to show their seriousness.

They can keep the charade up for some time and steal larger items. Mostly it's food, stuff to wear, or shiny things. As time progresses they'll escalate their aggressive behaviour and become violent.

- Alec

Spiderling

Known location: villages in following kingdoms: Paradrax, Neira, Bodera, and Kolridge.

Type: Arachnoid.

Weaknesses: Fire is very effective, but arrows, bullets, and weapons will kill them as well. These require higher skill though as spiderlings are agile.

Firstly, it's important to differentiate between spiderlings and needlers. Though they are the same beast, the spiderling is a young needler, a child of sorts. Their behaviour is very different, and therefore are often treated as two completely different beasts.

Spiderlings often reside in human households, though never more than one spiderling as they are territorial towards others of their kind. They carry this trait with them into adulthood. Spiderlings have sixteen long legs, helping them manoeuvre quickly. The body consists of two parts, the head and the thorax with all internal organs. Twelve legs are attached to the thorax and the last four on the sides of the head. Those legs are smaller and often used for detection in dark areas. The spiderling has five eyes, placed in a circle on the head. This gives them vision of all their surroundings. Normal spiders have fangs, but spiderlings have small, serrated teeth. The behaviour of spiderlings is often compared to that of a puppy. They hide from the residents of the house and steal food here and there. Spiderlings eat about anything, and as they grow, potentially even the family pet. Cats, small dogs, or terriers are often eaten. Wealthy households own many cats to more easily spot the intrusion of a spiderling in their house. The beasts are also fond of playing, and in early stages will occasionally play with pets, if there are any. It's also common for spiderlings to steal objects, and it's believed they do this to cause discontent to the owners.

As the spiderling continues to grow, their behaviour changes. They become sinister, their only objective to sate their hunger. Their body size increases, but what grows most are their legs, which end up being disproportionately long compared to the rest of their body. These legs become stiff, and sharp as steel and are used as lethal weapons in adulthood. When the spiderling has trouble fitting and moving freely in the house, they become dangerous. They murder the residents and eat them, before moving into the wild. It's common for spiderlings in their final state to take to the wild, and they seem to prefer to live in forests. From that point on they are referred to as needlers. Most of them will find their way to Bodera, the Mud-lands, where they are a huge problem. Exactly why so many of them end up there is unknown, but it's speculated it has something to do with their origins.

- Alec

Trollman

Known location: Typically found deep in the great forests of Varnat, though sightings of the creature have been reported in other regions too. These creatures are rare and seldom cross paths with humans.

Type: Large, humanoid, nocturnal.

Weaknesses: Weak and slow during the day, but extremely dangerous during the night. Tough skin, need concentrated fire or large strong weaponry, like ballistae, cannons, or other such devices to do any real damage.

Trollmen come from regular men or women, but more often men as typically more men are hunters, trackers, foresters, and the likes.

They're created in the forests because of a dangerous moss growing in caves. The moss is full of tiny sharp needles pointing in every direction. The typical assumed scenario is that a man seeks shelter in a cave during the night or heavy rainfall. While in the cave, he leans or steps on the moss growing on walls, roof, and the floor. The needles push through the skin and loosen before flowing into the bloodstream.

After this, the transformation begins. This event has not been witnessed and is discussed extensively amongst professionals on how it works. The first theorized bodily change is rapid vein expansion. Through some unexplained process, the blood radically changes its properties, including its colour, which turns dark-green. The subject grows to three times their size, turning their skin yellow and losing most of their hair. Most trollmen have patches of hair growing in random places. The nose becomes longer and points downwards, giving a great sense of smell. Feet and hands grow large, ending up looking disproportional to their already great size.

A newly created trollman seems to have no recollection of his/her previous life. During the day, it will merely roam purposelessly in the woods in a dull and unresponsive manner. They're said to be of no danger during daytime and people have been known to approach and touch them without causing any reaction. If a trollman is spotted during the day, make sure to be as far away from it as possible come nightfall. That is when they become dangerous. The trollman will become active and turn into a ferocious hunter. They will kill and eat anything they come across. There are stories of them even attacking boulderbeasts without hesitation. By night they're silent, strong, and fast, a deadly combination. If you ever find yourself up against a trollman, it's strongly advised not to attack them, as their heightened sense of smell and the ability to see clearly in darkness makes them almost impossible to kill.

- Khendric

Trashers

Known location: All kingdoms. Lives in large cities and most villages.

Type: Common, non-lethal.

Weakness: General weapons.

Trashers are a common sight in capital cities and many larger villages. They're thought to be the lesser kin to gremliks, but this is not known for certain. They're smaller than gremliks, with three fingers on each hand, one thumb, and two long fingers, each with a minor talon. They have bulging, grey bodies, though some have a green hue.

Trashers get their name from their behaviour: they look through people's trash for scraps of food and clothing. They don't care for everyday valuables, and it appears the trasher with the most items of clothing holds the highest rank. Trashers often run around in packs, playing and going through trash together. There are no known records of a trasher killing or even harming a human. It seems they'll flee a potential fight. Very few people mind trashers. Sometimes kids play with them, and they're known to provide some comedic value to the communities they inhabit, through quarrels with each other.

If a population grows too large, they get angry and kill each other off. This makes them a self-regulating species. Trashers are known to sometimes join in conversations, forming simple sentences. This makes them far superior in intelligence compared to their assumed kin, the gremliks. They often seek out conversation with people, as they seem to enjoy the company of humans.

- Alec

Wretcher

Known location: Major forests, grasslands, and mountain areas in Sangerian Grasslands, Ponteria, Norda and Ravens Hollow.

Type: Rare, aggressive, undead.

Weakness: Fire burned from pharlanax dust can kill it. If that is not available, fire will ward against it.

Wretchers are dangerous creatures, often compared to wolves, though they're not related. This comparison is brought to life because of their appearance in the dark of night, as they bear resemblance to a large canine.

A wretcher is larger than a wolf, with four legs, each paw having six toes. The claws are doubled, meaning each toe contains two smaller claws, one always touching the ground and one directly above. Their fur has a dark-blue hue, matching their blue eyes. The eyes of a wretcher emanate a thin luminescent smoke, making them easy to spot at night. What really makes their appearance menacing are their mouths. The prime characteristic of a wretcher's mouth is the overabundance of teeth, not placed in the regular pattern of wolves, but everywhere on and behind their jawline. The teeth grow uncontrollably, pointing in every direction with no discernible pattern. They lose teeth all the time, though this disadvantage is mitigated by rapid and constant regrowth.

One might wonder at this beast's 'undead' categorisation, given it behaves much like other predatory beasts and is dependent on sustenance for survival. What makes them undead is the fact that a wretcher won't become skinnier due to starvation but will rather decay. Their skin and intestines rot at a slow pace. Observations claim that it starts with the skin under the fur, often revealing the wretchers insides. As the wretcher starves, its ears and jaw begin to rot, then its tail and legs. It will eventually die as many of the vital organs decompose and cease to function.

Whatever you do, do not walk carelessly close to a severely rotten wretcher, as this is when they're at their most dangerous and unpredictable due to the ravenous hunger. They can summon incredible strength at the sight of living flesh when close to death.

Killing a wretcher is extremely difficult, and the only proven method is with the use of burning pharlanax dust. As this substance is even rarer than wretchers, a better method is to lock it up and starve it. If that is not an option, they usually shy away from fire, though there have been reports of wretchers attacking despite of it. It's suspected those wretchers did so because of starvation.

- Alec

Gorewing

Known location: The Mountainlands of Harrendale

Type: Flying, rare, dangerous.

Weakness: Weak to gunfire and general attacks to its back, due to the fact the skin on the back is soft. In contrast, the underbelly is covered in thick skin that is difficult to penetrate.

The gorewings are terrible beasts and often leave a mess after a meal—hence the name. A gorewing's figure resembles that of a giant bat, but it sports six legs instead of two. Their arms are modified into wings and are proportionally a lot weaker than the legs. Their skin resembles that of a snake, but thicker. The six legs each hold four sharp talons. Their eyes are small and completely black. It's the mouth that makes them look menacing, being a complete circle, from under their eyes to where the chin should be. It's filled with teeth descending down the throat in rows of concentric circles.

The gorewing kills its prey by slamming its head and teeth into it repeatedly until crushed. The talons on the two foremost legs are used to shred the prey. It's easy to spot a gorewing as it hovers above the ground, with their signature bat look, but with the tail at the end.

The gorewing isn't known to attack beasts close to their size or larger, instead feeding on those smaller than them. They have never been recorded attacking a varghaul for example, but sheep, humans, and the likes are among its usual prey.

After killing its prey, it sucks its meal up the oesophagus in the centre of the circular mouth, and into the stomach. On their backs are small openings in the skin that function as vents. The power of the suction is incredible and is rumoured to have enough power to empty the insides of its prey before it's even dead.

- Alec

Morgal

Known location: No specific location.

Type: Multiple bodies, hard to kill.

Weakness: Piercing their true heart.

To my knowledge, nobody knows how a morgal is born or comes into existence. One day, it just wakes up, at which point it is wearing the body of someone who has died prematurely. This cycle then repeats countless times. When its host body dies, it's reborn again as someone else who died prematurely, close to where its real heart is. The morgal seems to live with some injuries that the person who died might have had before death occurred, like missing limbs. To put this in perspective: if someone loses both hands and bleeds out, the morgal who wakes up with the body will continue to bleed from those same wounds. The morgal can die from this but wake up as someone new. It doesn't reincarnate as people who have died of old age, only those whose life has ended prematurely. The reason for this will, until further research has been done, only be speculation.

Every morgal has a true heart—which is black—that keeps beating despite not being connected to any blood vessels or tissue. This heart is both their life source and anchor. Wherever the heart lays, that is where they will revive after death. Exactly how close a corpse has to be for this to work is uncertain, but whatever is behind this mysterious process seems to have a reasonably good range. It is said the morgal is drawn towards the heart, always knowing where it is. They can hear the heartbeat of the black heart no matter where they are.

To kill a morgal, one must locate its heart and stab it. It's unknown if the morgal will live on after that, if already in a living body. I will need to find sources to confirm or deny either of those theories. Killing the morgal's current body will only inconvenience it until it finds its way back to where it was killed, if that is its desire.

Side note: Morgals aren't necessarily evil beasts. Often they seem to just wake up and try to live a normal life. Make sure you have a good talk with a morgal before deciding to kill it. Maybe it can be of help.

- Khendric

AUTHOR'S NOTE

This book actually exists because I was working on a larger project and a friend told me about a website where he was publishing books frequently, and I felt the urge to do the same. I put away the larger project and began writing this simple novel, which I thought would take around two months—my summer vacation. Oh, what a fool I was. Now, three years, three editors, four courses, one writing convention, and 16 beta readers later, it has become three novels, and I am finally ready.

Ara holds a place in my heart, because she's my first character to go through so much change—yet she feels so real. I hope you enjoy my work.

STAY IN TOUCH

Thank you so much for reading *The Beast Hunters*, the first book in *The Beasthunter of Ashbourn* series. If you enjoyed the first book in the series, and want a free short story about Khendric and Topper, as well as news about my author life, offers, and releases, you can sign up here:

https://www.authorcalende.com/newsletter-signup
Facebook: www.facebook.com/christer-Lende-108798154062930
Twitter: twitter.com/ChribsterL
Author website: www.authorcalende.com/
Instagram: www.instagram.com/christerlende

ABOUT THE AUTHOR

Christer Lende began writing in a library, which sounds fitting, only he was supposed to be there working on his engineering degree. He is a professional screenwriter, working with the Norwegian movie producer behind 'One Love,' 'Who Killed Birgitte?' and 'All About my Father', Bjørn Eivind Aarskog. Together, they are developing the manuscript for a Norwegian thriller. Bjørn hired Christer after reading *The Beast Hunters*, trusting he could bring his vision to life.

Christer lives in what Norwegians call a city, but people from actual cities would call a town. Of proud Viking blood, he honours his ancestors by heroically sitting in front of a computer writing Fantasy and Science Fiction books. He believes in writing a little every day, through weekends, Christmas, New Year's Eve, even his own birthday. When he's not writing, he takes care of his two dogs and tries to broker peace with his girlfriend. He's often found at the gym, trying to compensate for his height issues, or lazily playing video games.

Christer did get that Master's degree in Electrical Engineering, despite procrastinating by writing fiction in the library, and works for a large IT firm, but writing and storytelling are his passions.

For more information, you can visit:
https://www.authorcalende.com/about.